WOKEN

a short story collection

Sue Hampton

TSL Publications

First published in Great Britain in 2017
By TSL Publications, Rickmansworth

ISBN / 978-1-911070-54-2

Cover:
Paula Watkins

Portrait photo:
Mikaela Morgan

DEDICATION

WOKEN is dedicated to the
Water Protectors at Standing Rock,
and closer to home, to Tina Louise Rothery,
Fracktivist Nana compelled by love to protect the future
– because I'm grateful for their selfless resistance,
mounted with dignity, spirit, courage and conviction.

CONTENTS

Reviews of the collection

In her latest enthralling anthology, Sue Hampton succeeds in doing what only the very best writers can do: transforming strangers on the page into people we know. Into people we are. Her fiction is a mirror held up to the human heart, and here we may all recognize ourselves. Another modern masterwork.

Rick Cross, Alabama, USA, NASA media writer and author of *Times Squared*

I cannot begin to tell you how much I loved these stories. Your style is gorgeous. I have to tell you, these are humblingly brilliant in conception and delivery.

Stephen Carver, Norwich, UK, Head of Online Courses at the Unthank School of Writing, reader/mentor for The Literary Consultancy, freelance editor, and cultural
historian, author of *Shark Alley: The Memoirs of a Penny-a-Liner*

Woken is a powerful, poignant range of stories that reflect the uncertain emotions and events of the present. Hidden within each one are elements that touch us, challenge us and make us question what is happening and how the direction of the future is continually altering. Thank you for the privilege of reading them.

Patrick Carroll, Head of English at Shaw Wood Academy, Doncaster, Yorkshire, UK

Introduction

It was only in September 2016 that TSL published my first collection of short stories for adults – after nearly thirty full-length novels, most of them for children or teenagers. I was deeply heartened by the fifty-five appreciative reviews of individual stories printed in *Ravelled*, and by fulsome praise of the whole collection. Such comments, many of them from authors, librarians or teachers, mean a great deal more to me than sales figures, which of course is just as well!

Since then, my appetite for the short story has kept me busy both as a reader and writer, and I knew soon after publication that there would be a follow-up collection. Again, I have aimed for diversity. I hope you will find lyricism but also a style that's spare and sharp; one story emulates Victorian elegance intercut with pithy modern vernacular. There's a fable amongst the many contexts that are both very real and acutely contemporary (inasmuch as the publication process allows). Some aspire to humour of a satirical kind but there's tenderness too; many made me cry.

Is *Woken* darker than *Ravelled?* I suspect the simple answer is yes, and perhaps inevitably so, given the increasing darkness around us. One story climaxes at the Women's March on London: Stand Up to Trump. My writing has always been the most active part of my activism for peace, human rights and the environment, and of a celebration of difference. Love *must* Trump Hate. It's the most powerful force we know and these stories are, in their different ways, full of it.

There's a short commentary at the end of each story about what inspired it and what it means to me.

I hope they mean something to you too.

https://www.suehamptonauthor.co.uk/

BLUE ON BLUE

I thoroughly enjoyed this feel good short story. Being a similar age to the characters Sue brings to life so wonderfully, I empathised with all their doubts and human frailties, and their desires to make a better world. This is a wonderfully uplifting tale and I urge you to read it.

Liz Carlton, Greens for Animal Protection, UK

A beautiful, evocative, uplifting, lyrical reminder that life is too short, so seize the moment! Although I read it some time ago, it has stayed with me, which is a mark of the power of the writing.

Sally Goodman, Environmental Consultant, North Yorkshire, UK

"That's why imagination rocks," I told her, forefinger to my head. "In here you got the wind in your sails." I loved this, my favourite line from Blue on Blue *and one that made my mind light up. This is a beautiful short story.*

Beverley Wong, Singer and teacher, London, UK

BLUE ON BLUE

Seventy-five years old and a newbie! I decided, as I walked from the station, that I liked that. I could hear my tiddler, Walter, giving the game away the previous Christmas: "Grandma, what are you up to now?"

Why it had taken all those years of paid-up membership for me to make it there in body rather than spirit, I couldn't have explained. It was just a weekend and the setting was beautiful. I only hoped nobody was waiting for me at that very moment in some café or committee meeting, because double bookings had become my speciality, much to the family's exasperation at times. Whatever, as the teenagers would say; it felt good to be close. The rain had cleared and the sun was so warm I almost wished I'd clicked on the camping option, ignoring the sensible voice that liked to remind me of the passage of time since I'd been under canvas and the stiff knees that might hold me captive in a tent. But not the cancer I'd outlived. It was Jen and Frannie who never let me forget that, as if the lost breast and the chemo had left me wispy and brittle too. The two of them had a habit of questioning the 'wisdom' of everything, especially the A word: activism. "I shan't be getting arrested," I'd told them, "not this weekend anyway." And of course I understand the way people sidestep, just for functioning's sake. But they know it's for them, and the grandchildren most of all.

I could have answered Walter's question with, "Trying to spare you, my darling, and others like you, who haven't trashed this beautiful Earth." Not yet anyway. But he'd just turned three, bless him. Never knew his grandfather; only two out of seven ever heard my Jack sing, "Hooray and up she rises!" as he lifted them up and over his head. There was something about June skies and scents that always reminded me of the burial, of losing Jack too soon. I'd been living for many decades with the expectation of sadness marbling through the beauty and I liked to think it no longer hurt – any more than autumns lost to winter, or blue skies cleared for rain.

As I crossed the field around the Youth Hostel, smiling at the goats with their heads down to the deep-green grass, I saw a decorated archway ahead and a textured tapestry of colour beyond. Already people were raising hands, smiling, saying hi. Children were running, some of them barefoot and one in patchwork dungarees with long, ribboned plaits bouncing. Son number one would have muttered about New Age hippies: patchouli, roll-ups, piercings, sweat, herbal tea and broccoli smoothies. But as I moved towards the marquee with its pinned notices flapping, I passed a retired headmaster type with round specs, skinny legs and a saw. He interrupted the tune he was whistling to volunteer that he was making a cocktail bar for later.

I noticed three young women sitting together on a straw bale, talking animatedly. One was in a hijab, with a silver stud on her nose that caught the sun and glittery bangles chinking. Next to her was a blonde who might, in her shorts and vest, have been stopping off on her way to a running track, her ponytail swinging as she turned towards a mixed-race beauty with a Hendrix halo of curls and a baby at her breast. Heartened to be double the average age and resisting the urge to scan the crowd for older, greyer and creakier women, I followed signs and registered.

The handbook offered a comprehensive schedule: politics, creativity, spirituality, veggie food and African music, with a couple of 'names' last seen on *Question Time* or a much bigger screen in Trafalgar Square at the end of a march. Excited, I told the girl behind the school table in the entrance hall that it all looked wonderful.

"Anything missing?" she asked.

"Tap dancing?" I suggested, and smiled because she wasn't sure how to react. She couldn't know that I'd loved that even longer than hockey and swimming, and spent Sunday afternoons as a teenager in front of Fred Astaire musicals copying the moves.

"Maybe next year," I quipped.

I was hungry already. "Maybe you should eat more cake," the nurse had said at my check-up. Justified, I was led by temptation towards a purple tent with tassels around the edge, a shady floor of Moroccan cushions and curly pink chalk letters advertising 'cool creamy halva shake (vegan)'.

"Leroy Jonelle?" I heard, turning. A tight white Oxbridge voice, but I didn't see where it came from right away. The boy had harem pants and flip-flops, with hair as silky and abundant as mine was thin and corkscrewed.

"Yeah, man," I said, hand outstretched, and he gave it a slap so quick I thought he must be red-hot at ping pong. "Have we met?"

"Nah," he answered. "I just read your badge. I might come along though. Eden, Eden Joy. Poetry's part of it, right?"

I could have said, "All!" But he was on the move anyway, spotting friends, accelerating.

It took a while but I found it in the programme. *Peace through self-expression: a creative workshop with performance poet Leroy Jonelle.* I'd grinned to myself first time I saw it. I didn't remember giving anyone that wording, and truth was I hadn't written anything for a while. Plus I preferred *eco poet*, partly because I hadn't performed for a while either. Looking at all the young people around me, I figured they'd be hoping for someone hip, with a bare brown six-pack and braided heavyweight hair. Not an old guy like me, with no more on top than a monk in medieval paintings and a note stitched into my backpack reminding me: *Heart pills.* Ten years earlier I'd cycled all the way from York to Castleton. I could see that as shit happening but I preferred to think of it as progress towards peace.

As I sat on the steps in front of the house, the song from back in the day began to play in my head: *Young at Heart* by The Bluebells. I used to sing it to the ocean and the wind when I worked the boats, blue on blue, with no clue where the world was heading. Now I was a long way from the Caribbean and I wouldn't be flying back, not unless they made airplanes carbon-free before I passed. But England was home and these were my people. Den, Yusuf, Bella and Chaz, Mia and Suzie, Haresh, Tony – I'd already seen them all, hugged, had my back slapped, told them I was 'good'. It was Haresh who'd said, "Yeah, you will be, bro. I'm coming. Tomorrow morning, yeah?"

Yeah. Only I had no clear idea what form the creativity would take. Which, to quote young Eden Joy (whose name was creative in itself), was part of it, right?

The first fracktivism workshop must be starting soon. I checked. Yurt 3, back over the little bridge and through the gate.

There were a couple of Nanas in their yellow pinnies already sitting in the middle of the horseshoe when I arrived and took a seat near the opening. I recognised the shorter of the two from social media, a heroine of mine.

I'd seen her best our revered Chancellor, and replayed it on YouTube more than once, punching the air with every victory.

"Hiya," she said with a smile, tapping her pen on a fat spring file. "You all right, love?"

"Fine thanks," I said, without admitting that I couldn't feel more awestruck if I'd just met Mo Farah or Meryl Streep. She might be a granny but she was at least ten years younger than me. Even as she swung one leg over another and twitched her bare toes in her sandals I could see her energy, feel it. Her commitment. I felt shadowy, greyer than my hair. We were Facebook friends, but she had no reason to know me – unlike the middle-aged trio who bundled in and embraced her.

"Where you from?" her friend asked me. I saw Frack-Free Notts in red on the yellow pinny.

"Essex," I said. "Not the frontline. But I want to be ready."

More takers for the workshop were filing through. We swapped names as the yurt filled up.

"Come and sit with us, Cherry," my heroine said, and her friend added, "Yeah, come on, duck."

But I had so much gubbins – fat old rucksack, my favourite velvet bag just because my Joanna chose it for my seventy-fifth birthday, bless her, and my programme and glasses and the pen and notebook I'd already dug out – that by the time I'd managed to collect it all up, someone the Nanas knew better had slipped in unencumbered and taken the seat on offer. "Leroy, my love!" I heard, and "It's my favourite wordsmith!"

He was basketball-tall and lean. From the back, and the way he walked, he could have been fifty-odd, but his smile made more creases than that and his teeth were less than complete. It was a grin I might call cheeky on a boy, or mischievous. His outdoor skin gave no slack and his hair was crispy, a domed brown scalp showing through.

My vacated seat now taken, I took the one next to him.

"Cherry, meet Leroy Jonelle."

"Hi, Cherry. How you doin'?"

The voice was deep but with a papery crackle that made the question sound playful – and another smile came with it. I didn't get the chance to answer, though, because the workshop leaders said they'd like to make a start. We all watched the last couple of seats filled by apologetic

14

latecomers. *Fracking: the story so far*, I wrote, and underlined it with a wavy squiggle. I might not have much to contribute, but I had plenty to learn.

It was mostly veterans: Horse Hill, Balcombe, Ryedale, Fylde, people with stories to tell. So the introductions around the yurt took a while.

Then I heard on my left, "Cherry Garnet, Essex. Nothing to report, I'm afraid, except ignorance and well, fear." She spoke very quietly, almost like an apology. I thought she was one of those women who can't help saying sorry even when you tread on their toes. Right away people jumped in, telling her *you learn fast in this business* and *we're all afraid of fracking, that's why we're here.* Then, before I could take my turn, she added, straightening up a bit, "But they're not going to get away with it. I know that much." Except that it was a kind of throwaway so only a couple of us heard enough to cry, "Yeah!" She gave me an embarrassed kind of smile. I guessed she was my generation but I could picture her as a girl, when her long plait wasn't white.

When we had to split into groups she kept her head down a lot, scribbling away. I don't do notes, just questions. I thought: teacher, probably a Shakespeare fan but in love with Mr Darcy like all very-English women. I wrote a poem about that once, a kind of warm-up for gigs, but I wasn't sure it would impress her. Or me, nowadays. There was a point when she caught me watching her spot-pointing her notes and murmured, "You'll remember all this?"

"Mainly those grandkids," I said, "turning to lobsters in the bathwater."

I wanted to tell her I had no more credits to my name than she did, unless you counted the poem I'd read for YouTube over images that spoke for themselves – and a junior Jonelle should have been ahead of my name because he wasn't so much crew as captain. "You still got it," he told me as he worked his technical magic, and I knew what *that* meant.

After the workshop finished I looked at Cherry Garnet packing up, and figured she was a lost opportunity, a gap. Or even an illusion. Because all she'd shown from seven decades of living on this Earth was for others: admiration, concern and a kind of grief. And I like uncovering the buried people. Resurrecting them, if you like.

"It's kind of early to eat," I began, "but …"

"Not for me," she said. "I get up at five."

So we strolled down to the canteen, and she told me she loved tap dancing, back in the day. But when I asked for a step or two on the concrete while we queued, she looked at her sandals and shook her head so her plait swayed.

"That's O.K. I can imagine those feet in action," I said.

"Well it wouldn't be poetry in motion. Not anymore."

"That's why imagination rocks," I told her, forefinger to my head. "In here you got the wind in your sails."

We both went for baked beans with our potatoes, but Leroy piled on cheese and added a last-minute veggie burger. I didn't really want to have the vegan conversation, the transport vs diet debate as if it's either/or when it has to be all. Not just because it feels like point-scoring but because I didn't want to be disappointed in Leroy Jonelle, or anyone there. I hate fault-finding even more than halo-polishing. As we sat down with our cutlery I heard someone behind us say, "It's a political act, every time you eat," and Leroy grinned at me. So I thought maybe he was as carefree as he looked, deep down, in spite of fracking and melting ice – couldn't help himself, maybe.

"Is that how you see it?" he asked.

"I've never been political. I used to think it was tribal and dishonest. A surrender of the light inside. You know, like soldiers having to obey orders regardless of what that light tells them."

He nodded as if that thought was new. "But now your inner light has guided you to …?"

"It's brought me here," I said. "To learn what more I can do and be." The kind of words I only think, or type. Not say out loud to strangers.

"Yeah," he said. "I like the being – kinda more than the doing." I nodded and he smiled. "Making an exception of eating, though, especially baked beans."

I laughed. It was the boyishness of it, and the smile in the brown eyes. So why did I turn it, telling him that after Jack died, beans on toast and red wine became my default option as main meal of the day? I suppose because I wanted the poet to read me – not just the outer layers but the core. That was how he made me feel. And maybe there was an unacknowledged sleuth in me that wanted to know whether anyone loved him, kept him warm at night – the way I thought I might like to do.

He asked and I gave him the numbers: widowed at sixty-eight just before our forty-sixth anniversary, a heart attack. I didn't expect tears, few and brief as they were, to break in on proceedings. I didn't expect his hand on my upper arm – luckily not the site of the melanoma scar which was still a bit sore. He felt very warm.

He hadn't said much, but he looked as if he saw. Me, I mean. Or the human condition, maybe both. Then I apologised.

"I've overloaded you!"

"I like overload," he said, glancing at his potato, buried under a cheese mountain and a baked bean sea. "But I'm sorry you've been so sad."

"You're not … grieving?"

"Not for a partner. I never married. I have a nephew who has the coolest kids but none of my own."

"No?" What do you say? This was a life so unlike mine.

"Let a good woman go when I cared more for my freedom. Just like my daddy before me. Which probably spared us both divorce but makes the pair of us damn fools." His shoulders dropped. "For sure."

He told me about leaving his old dinghy named Melody, "moored and bobbing for weeks on end" to skipper boats for rich people who owned or hired them but didn't know what to do with them. "When you think about all the shit going down on land it's kind of a screwed way to live. But me, the sea and Melody …" He paused, as if this was the first line in a verse. "Don't buy no bread." He said he sold the dinghy and came over to the U.K. when a new century on the horizon woke him up from what he called his "snoozing". His mother was here and needed him. "I was a late learner," he said.

"But the poems were always there?"

"Yeah. Like a glimpse, a rustle, you know? A burst of sun. No big picture, nothing connecting the breaths."

"Like God?" I suggested.

"Is that what you call it?"

"Sometimes," I said, "yes. But it's always the light."

"And there have to be shadows."

"Oh yes," I said, "of the valley of death." Something made me laugh. "Don't let me stop you eating!"

17

"You can't!" He mopped up sauce with his potato skin. "I'm not afraid of the dying itself, the passing. I think of it like floating, but still. Blinking away the last sunlight, lost to the wind." He wiped his mouth with a napkin. "You?"

"I try not to think of it at all," I said, "because I can't leave this mess behind me. Maybe that's why I'm an old radical – just when I'm too feeble to make it count."

"Feeble's not the word I'd choose."

I waited, but he didn't supply another. Or at least, he might have, if some people he knew hadn't joined the food queue and hailed him.

"Please," I said, "go and see your friends. I'm a slow eater these days."

It was the opposite of what I wanted, but I set him free – slipping away a few moments later to exit by the other door. I was afraid to monopolise him but more afraid of staying to hear him say, *"Well, see you around."* Walking faster than I usually did and wondering whether he had looked for me yet, I tried to imagine the expression on his face and all I pictured was curiosity. I told myself not to be a fool. No distractions and no fantasies please. And in my head I heard, "Mum, what are you like?" but I couldn't even be sure which of the four had asked the question.

Even when they frustrate the hell out of me, I like people. I'm in awe of human energy, and that respect grows as fast as mine wilts. I got me a shortage. But there's something beautiful about the way we can be when we're together in the quietness, just being – like the trees and the grass, and the fish in the pond by Reception and the bubbles around them. There can be five hundred of us, scattered through a space as green and cherished as this one, and voices threading through like the bodies on the move, but the peace doesn't break. It holds us all. It's a unity of purpose for sure, because we're all there for the same reasons, but it's deeper than that. It's a species thing. Without our own domestic boxes and workplaces, our routines and rituals, we're just humans. No strutting or footstamping or beating our chests. We're just glad to connect in the web of life. I sat on a bale with my eyes closed and thought about my workshop the next day. "Your senses are superpowers," I'd tell them, counting on them finding the same place. And knowing I was lucky to go there, day after day, wherever.

I wasn't sure how much peace Cherry Garnet found, or gave herself. I figured she was grieving for the world and her helplessness in it, but I was hoping I could help her to feel her strength. Breathe it. I would have been glad if I'd opened my eyes to find her folding her skirt to join me on the straw. But I couldn't see her anywhere.

I soon got talking to some guys who remembered me.

"Hey," said one. "Not dead yet. Cool."

When you're the oldest black guy on a march you make an impression. Especially if you're carrying a placard that says READY TO DIE one side and on the other, a photo of some indigenous peoples building walls to keep out rising seas: BUT THEY'RE NOT.

The new wave of activists is so young, fired up, but committed to non-violence too. Yeah, I like people. I knew I liked Cherry Garnet a lot.

I disciplined myself and focused. There was an inspiring talk in the marquee, with campaigners from all over the world reporting good news – like mayors of cities taking action when governments are too slow, and all kinds of movements growing in the same cause. I spotted Leroy on the other side of the tent but I didn't attempt eye contact. I had an idea his vision wasn't eagle-sharp; with me it's the ears that really let me down at times but here the speakers all had microphones. Then I moved on to a workshop about Muslim Climate Action, welcomed by a beautiful young woman who handed over to a "wise and great inspiration." He seemed to be leading like Pope Francis and at much the same sort of age. Leroy must have been in one of the other yurts, or chilling under a tree. There was so much on offer and I realised I was tiring already.

After a cup of tea I took myself into the craft tent to make a dream catcher, taught by a pierced young mum my own daughters would call 'grungy' – although Frannie at least would be envious of the lilies tattooed on her muscular left leg. Tia was very patient with my deafness and clicky old fingers that don't always bend or keep control. My willow frame wasn't very circular, and I broke my all-natural vow with coloured pipe cleaners and a few sequins that eventually settled to wink on the wood. But it was a joy to feel childlike, investigating the possibilities with sticks and pine cones, ferns and feathers. As I played I listened to the others – all younger, faster and freer – while looking up and out from time to time, in case Leroy Jonelle strolled on by.

Tia noticed and asked if I was with anyone. I didn't want to talk death or loneliness so I just said no, and tried not to sound sorry about it.

"Guys don't always understand," said Tia. She looked at a Pre-Raphaelite little girl in a Snow White dress and small Doc Martens, chasing around the straw bales after a boy in a spotty sunhat and baggy shorts. "I had to cut loose from her dad."

I made sympathetic noises. I supposed Jack had cut loose from me, and remembered Leroy's idea about dying: floating but still, blinking away the last sunlight. I felt widowed again. Two of the women reached out to each other with their free hands, and squeezed.

"We're a couple," one said, and the other added, "and we mostly understand."

I smiled and Tia cried, "Girl power!" Then she looked at my dream catcher so I said, "I'm afraid it's not very successful. Or attractive."

"Fuck attractive," said Tia. "Fuck successful. I love it, it's got character. It's individual. Be proud." The others were agreeing. "Excuse the language. My gran doesn't like it."

"Don't worry," I said, thinking that I was with her gran in principle but sometimes the word was the only one that did the job. "I think maybe I'll call this finished now."

She hung it for me and took a photo on her phone.

"Thanks, Cherry," she told me, adding that it was lovely to meet me and she wished her gran was a warrior too.

I thanked her back and left the tent with a smile for my highly individual artwork, which swung in the breeze and nudged its more conventional neighbours. But I felt a bit of a fraud all the same.

I was going to introduce the guys to Cherry but she vanished. Her choice but I regretted mine. She must have checked in to a different yurt when I picked Permaculture. I could imagine her gardening – if her knees allowed – and figured any seed would thrive with her in charge. Then I thought maybe those grandkids kept her too busy with a different kind of nurturing.

I like an afternoon nap when I can and I was missing the regeneration so I went to the Chill Zone in the Lounge, where the curtains billowed around the open French doors. I found a middle-aged woman reading a book and a young guy lying on the floor with his hands open on each side, receiving. I just chose an old sofa and curled my legs up. Not really expecting to sleep, just thinking – about the pattern of the wooden floor, the grain and the angles, the texture of the curtains that had probably been there since the Eighties, the movement in the Cézanne tree-scape through the large bay window. And Cherry Garnet, who liked to be real until she held back and left me guessing.

It was after six when I woke, shook myself out of the stiffness and joined the Dance workshop late. Four guys and a dozen women but she wasn't one of them. My Water moves felt good and slow, but when we switched to Fire I sat and watched. Humans can flame and maybe I used to, now and then. I managed a spark or two. But Earth is hard to be if you get rock-bound and forget the life that teems, the roots that spread.

I left the others to that challenge and hoped I'd meet Cherry in the Canteen, but I missed her. She wasn't in Cloud Appreciation, either, but I memorised the names to tell her, wrote them in the air and said them out loud to hold onto them: words like *nimbostratus, altocumulus, noctilucent, tropospheric, nacreous.* In my head I asked her how comes I didn't know all this, after all the days and nights I'd watched the skies from some deck or other, blue on blue? In my head I told her human ignorance knows no bounds. Mine, anyways.

But she didn't appear for the African drumming, and the healthy booze-free cocktails didn't tempt her. Around ten thirty, I started shipping water during a debate about electric cars – on account, I guess, of me never owning anything with more wheels than a bike. I went up to fit my earplugs in my YHA bedroom, realising I didn't even know where she was sleeping.

"Foolish, Leroy," I murmured to myself, and shifted the lumps around my pillow.

I lost sleep at the B&B, which I hadn't understood was a pub. Comfortable as it was, my room looked down on the entrance, and the tables facing the narrow village street. And the fire doors slammed and clunked at both ends of the corridor, as if they needed to seal it airtight. In the end I got up, made myself black tea and read my notes on the refugee crisis, trying to digest them in case anyone, including Leroy Jonelle, asked questions, but not sure whether they'd hold up for presenting to the Green Party meeting or the town's One World committee. Underlining phrases like *Climate change refugees* and shaking my head because of dots so close together they almost joined up when no one was looking. There had been a point when the writing faltered on the page because the horror broke through, too big to shape. Not because of the millions, even though at the time I asked for the figure to be repeated in case I'd misheard – because numbers can't do it, only one human story. I felt ashamed that after that I jumped right back into my own. But reprimanding myself didn't seem to be working. Recklessness was long overdue. And Leroy Jonelle was eighty-one years old.

Dear Leroy, I wrote. *Between us we've clocked up more than a hundred and fifty years of life with no way of knowing how much or how little more there is to come. So in my head I hear 'Carpe Diem' and there's just the one before we part company. I haven't written a note of this kind since I was fourteen and smitten with my friend's boyfriend's friend, who wasn't, it turned out, smitten with me. I would like to stay in touch and see you again, if you would like that too, but if not, I wish you happiness and peace and please do wave if you see me on a demonstration.* I added my mobile number and email address. Then I signed it, minus the automatic kiss.

I folded it, wrote his name on the front and went back to bed with no idea when to hand it over. Somehow I slept after that, and in my dreams Leroy was there to rescue drowning children. I woke to sunshine, felt grateful for my shower and leisurely breakfast and watched the door as guests joined me in the dining room. Most of them were heading back to camp too.

"He loved it," said the mother of a child in a high chair. "Made friends right off. Got dirtier than usual, mind."

A middle-aged couple sat at my table and we shared what we'd learned and done. May was a retired teacher who spent most of breakfast enjoying the toddler, and Harry a floppy-haired Methodist minister and Reiki master. They were part of Operation Noah and intent on greening the church in spite of certain members making it clear that "solar panels would only be fitted over their dead bodies".

"Wouldn't that make them a bit bumpy?" I quipped, and Harry laughed too loudly and long to speak. When he'd recovered and I'd poured more coffee, May produced the programme and I said I might join them at the multi-faith open air service. I pointed to Leroy's workshop which would follow.

"Oh, he's a delight!" cried May. "We were chatting last night. Harry's committed to Shared Housing at eleven but I might not be able to resist."

She gave me a very surreptitious wink.

I looked out at the blue sky and wished, when they asked about my train home, that I hadn't chosen the 15:40. My note was in the pocket of my velvet bag but at that point I couldn't imagine how to deliver it. My fourteen-year-old self could delegate that job to my friend, who'd reported back that the object of my crush "just laughed, and swore". I told myself it was time to learn my lesson, and spare myself humiliation. Before I checked out of the pub, I very nearly dropped it in the wastepaper basket. But I didn't.

I used to sleep upright, in clothes, by daylight – any time I fancied a cat nap. These days the nights get broken up into episodes and the dreams take me back further than I knew I remembered. Antigua as it used to seem when I was knee-high. Before I know it I'm back at school: the yard where we raced and chased each other barefoot without rules, the yam dinners, the squeak of chalk and a map of the world mostly coloured red. And Gramps meeting me when the bell rang, as if he'd just been rattled awake. Walking home at his pace, with him always stopping to sit on the same stump and light roll-ups, took even longer than the Morning Prayers we recited in our rows.

When I opened my eyes that morning I didn't compute the Youth Hostel right away. Things take time; I'm like Gramps now but I get there in the end. A workshop at eleven in the Lounge. What was that title again?

I figured there was no need to check the time, just the light and what I called its texture. But it turned out that I was at the tail end for breakfast. The canteen clock said ten fifteen as I ladled my baked beans and mushrooms onto soft toast and poured my coffee black. A couple of delicate, serious-looking girls at my table had started their morning with multi-faith worship which they said was "beautiful", "intimate". "We're Buddhists," one added. I nearly asked them whether Cherry, who sometimes called the light God, had been there. But how would I describe her, apart from her age? Slim, with an abundance of silvery hair? Looks like a cellist, or a guide at a National Trust garden? Probably guarded her own silence with smiles, and quietly thanked everyone when the hour was up?

I'd left my programme in my room but the door to the Lounge had my name on it. *Peace through self-expression: a creative workshop*. My brain knew I'd done this before, or something very like it, but it couldn't recall exactly what or how. The previous group began to leave, some of them looking familiar from the night before as they said my name. One middle-aged, bearded guy slapped my back and told me cheerfully, "Break a leg." The sun was blazing in but most of the windows resisted when I tried to throw them all wide open to the breeze. I couldn't believe the heat that had got inside my body.

One by one, then two by two, people joined me, depositing rucksacks and holdalls, removing hats and sunglasses. All of them, I figured, expecting more than I could think to deliver. Including Eden Joy, who greeted me like a gramps he hadn't seen for a while. I smiled, tried to collect the other names that were a lot harder to hold without spilling, and invited people to chill. They'd all found sofa, floor or armchair space when Cherry walked in.

"Cherry, hey!" I cried.

"Hello, Leroy," she said, and took the largest armchair, which would have accommodated two of her. Then, as I redirected a woman who wanted *LGBTQ: celebrating difference*, I found Cherry Garnet padding towards me with something in her hand.

"This is for you," she said, as if delivering on a promise. "For later," she added, as I looked at my name in big, arty letters with tails that flourished. So I slipped it in the back pocket of my long shorts, wondering how I was going to recover any plan I might once have had now that her handwriting was nestling there.

"Welcome," I said. The sweat on the top of my head felt cool. "To what I hope will be a celebration of the gifts we bring, as creative beings." And, suddenly inspired, I began with the cave painting poem. But I never finished it.

I had my eyes closed at the start of Leroy's poem because I wanted to picture what the words painted, not his smile or my note wadding in his back pocket. At the thud I opened them to find him on the floor, face down.

I heard, "You all right, dude?" "He's fainted, it's the heat" and "It could be his heart" as I hurried to feel his forehead and find a pulse. I wasn't good at this. And the last time I'd checked these things, Jack was dead under our duvet.

"Somebody call the paramedics," I said.

He was so warm; this time they might not be too late. Someone who looked like a schoolgirl to me said her friend was a medical student just back from the Calais Jungle and should be in Yurt 1.

"Yes, yes," I said. I'd tracked a heart rate that seemed too fast, too jumpy. She raced out through the French doors; a lad called Eden went to find one of the stewards; I heard someone get through on the phone, asking, "Where is this place again?" and I knew the postcode, don't ask me why. I held one hand and stroked the beads of perspiration from Leroy's head. That was when the word surfaced, the four-letter one I'd been knocking back. *I think I love you*, I told him, in the silence that connected us. His hair felt a little scratchy. The curls were so tight.

"You'll be all right, Leroy," I murmured. "Don't start floating yet."

The young woman passed her phone to me and I realised they all thought we were lovers. "Yes," I said, "Leroy Jonelle, aged eighty-one. Please hurry."

At first I listened for the sea. I looked for blue on blue. The light was bright and white, like the walls and the crisp sheet. I registered the uniforms but the clarity took its time coming, as if I was at the optician's and it was a while before they put the right lens in place. I heard her before I noticed her.

"He's awake." She was sitting with a book on her lap in the chair beside the bed.

"Cherry Garnet," I said, "Hey."

She touched my hand lightly, briefly, and rose to fetch a nurse. I couldn't quite figure it out: where I'd been and what happened, the date, the time, how long ... But this woman, looking so cool and loose and floral and calm, was the first thing I knew.

I found myself checked and questioned by a round-cheeked Spanish guy with a name too long and small for me to read, so he told me to call him Joe. Much better heart rate, he said, and blood pressure down. The doctor would be along soon, he told me brightly, but I was doing well and there were pills to take. Pills I'd better remember in future. I was grateful, but I was glad too when he left us – Cherry Garnet and me.

"They think we're married," she told me. She smoothed her long skirt which swung around her ankles. "I tried to tell them we only met yesterday." She smiled. "Without sounding like a hooker."

I have a big laugh. Everyone looked. The Lounge was coming back to me, with the parquet floor coated in dust and the cold droplets gathering on my head as the solid world shifted. "You gave me a note," I said, leaning out towards the bedside unit where I supposed my clothes must be.

"Read it when I've gone," she told me.

"You're leaving?" I couldn't think where she lived.

She shook her head and smiled. Her hand on my arm was cool. "I've no plans to go any further than the café. Not until they say you can go too."

"And then?" I took both her hands between mine so there'd be no gaps between the words for the meaning to slip through. "I have a tiny flat with a roof garden. And a view of the sea on a clear day. With my glasses on." She nodded; I must have told her this already. I figured she was the sort of woman who lets the other person talk. "But no second bedroom."

"Well …" she said, "That's not necessarily a problem." I looked, wanting to read her eyes, imagining how it would feel to kiss her mouth. She gave a different kind of smile. "In any case, I have a garden. And a spare bedroom full of teddies, board games and picture books, with a very large Gruffalo in residence."

I grinned. "Sounds great. Sounds like we have options." I sipped water, spilt it and reached for her again. "Cherry Garnet, are you really happening to me?"

"If you're happening to me, Leroy Jonelle."

I leaned towards her and she leaned too. I kissed her, hoping I didn't taste like a corpse. A chaste kiss but they can be sweet. That's something age teaches you.

"I am," I said.

We're going back this year, and Jen says we can take Walter with us. Leroy's talking about an open-air 'wedding' if the sun shines, blue on blue. No ceremony, just hand in hand with silence between us, and the straw bales behind us in case we need to sit. He wants to place flowers in my hair.

More about *Blue on Blue*

In June 2015 Leslie and I went to Friends of the Earth Basecamp at a Youth Hostel in Yorkshire, and found the experience creative, informative and inspiring. A few months later I planned a love story that begins even later in life than ours, and needed a vivid and unusual setting. Readers familiar with such events will recognise details I've taken from memory; others may gain insight into a way of thinking and being that a friend described as 'alternative'.

Like all the minor characters, Cherry and Leroy are entirely fictional. But we all know couples who've begun again, and people who've fallen for someone whose life experience and cultural background are very different from their own. When I hear that a friend's son or daughter has a partner from Japan, China, Nigeria, Estonia or Brazil, the hashtag #WeAreOne seems achievable. I only hope that air miles will soon be carbon-free.

After sending this story to a few friends, I was amused to receive two emails on the same day, from one reader telling me she'd cried and another that she was left with a big smile on her face. Then I realised that both responses were just what I intended. This story is happy – love is possible, nature is beautiful, the human spirit has strength in depth and there are people committed to working for change – and at the same time achingly sad. We die, and sometimes in the world love seems to be dying too. But it never does. That's the most important thing I've learned in sixty years: love is stronger than death.

LOST BOYS

Heartbreaking. A beautifully crafted arc of love, like a rainbow describing pain. In gentle accepting tones, we come to recognise a series of blessings disguised as tragedies and then we experience tragedy. I cried.

Tania Clarke, Psychotherapist and coach, Herts, UK

Like the stars referred to in the narrative, Sue Hampton's short story Lost Boys *shines. Packing one hell of a narrative into a few short pages, this is not just a moving story of family dynamics and inevitable loss, but a delving into the nature of individuality, the pressures of conventionality and how vulnerable the human spirit is to being crushed. A fable for modern times and a reminder that we're all star-shaped in our own way.*

Charlotte Reid, Writer and Director, GrafikLanguage Agency, Norwich, UK

I have no idea how I fell in love with four characters in so few words. What a powerful impact; I felt joy, sadness, regret (mainly on my part as a mother of boys) and fury at the current pressures teachers are put under by a diabolical education system.

Sally Newell, IT Support Helpdesk, Bucks, UK

Lost Boys *is a delightful and powerful story. It covers a lot of ground, taking the reader on an emotionally charged journey. We learn about the way in which family dynamics work, how a sibling like Bea has to grow up quickly when faced with the challenge of 'helping her brother', Jed. Then we feel her pain and sadness at the end. The story resonates strongly with me and I believe that this type of story can help others to understand a little of what it's like for a child with Autism/ADHD or any other cognitive disorder. Well done Sue Hampton. I love the way you write.*

Raine Geoghegan, MA, BA, Dip RWTA, Poet, Theatre Practitioner & founder of 'Writing from the Heart' a Creative Writing programme, Sussex, UK

A delightful short story that gives insight into the road to understanding someone whose outlook on life is a little different. I found the narrator Bea very engaging.

Robbie Cheadle, Associate Director, Deal Advisory,
Johannesburg, South Africa

LOST BOYS

My name is Bea and I've just started a Creative Writing degree at university. For my first assignment, I had to write a piece exploring my own experience from the inside, and my subject was obvious. Because I lost two boys at once.

When Jed was born I was jealous as hell. At two and a half I ruled the roost, especially with Grandma, who called me Queen Bee. I was the sort of little girl who wanted frills on the tops of my ankle socks and wouldn't wear them once the white dimmed. I made the rules in all my games and bossed all the players, but Granddad Ben was the most fun. If I wanted him to long jump in the garden, he'd rev up like a racing car and fly. If I needed him to be a lion, his ferocious pounce would have more spring than a beach ball, and when we danced he'd keep spinning and gliding long after I'd flopped onto the sofa. I didn't need a baby brother. Mum and Dad must have done their best to make the prospect sound exciting but I knew I didn't want to share anything I loved, especially Granddad.

Of course I don't remember it like a narrative in chapters, just Mum coming home from hospital with a package that wasn't a present. He didn't jump out of her arms and start to climb the curtains, not at first. But before long he'd amuse himself, even once he was wide awake, by bopping around in his cot and pulling things apart. I didn't appreciate that any more than his non-verbal commentary intercut with eruptions of laughter. He seemed like an animal to me, and I'd rather have a pet I could lock up in a cage. Soon Jed had escaped from the cot, and his room. He'd appear in mine when the world was still dark, climb onto my bed and laugh as he pulled my nose, ears or fingers, or helped my teddy to wake me up with a furry dance on my head. And very soon I'd had enough.

I don't think I was the only one struggling to manage life with a small but permanently elasticated human in the house. There was a weekend when Mum and Dad went away to the Cotswolds for a break from

Jumping Jed and left us with Grandma and Granddad. When we arrived, Grandma was waving at the kitchen window, but Granddad charged out of the front door with his fists pumping, just as an unclipped Jed hurled himself out of the car and raced down the path for a collision. By the time I joined them Jed was attached to Granddad like a backpack, with swinging legs and dancing arms.

Of course Grandma scooped me up and stroked the hair from my forehead so she could kiss it. Jed wasn't the only guest who had a wonderful stay. All the same, the story goes that when he played jack-in-the-box, curled up ready to eject, I ran to find some tape and cried, "Granddad, come on, let's stick down the flaps!" Not that any delivery box could contain my brother for long.

I was five or six when one Saturday in summer Grandma took the chance, after we'd slid our muffins into the oven, to explain. Granddad and Jed were doing something they called space athletics in the garden – which meant the kind of wildness that could only be excused by extra legs or a different kind of gravity.

Grandma made me a cup of milky grown-up tea, and we sat down at the kitchen table.

"Bea," she said, "I'm going to ask you to help Jed."

I'm sure that wasn't what I wanted to hear. Did she mean with his alien impressions or double-racket tennis, or just remembering not to kick his muddy trainers off against the wall? Grandma told me he was going to start school soon and he wasn't going to find it easy. I thought she meant Maths because I didn't like the tests myself.

"He may find it hard to fit in, Bea, and spend a lot of time in trouble."

"He could be more sensible," I said. I was proud that my teacher had used that word about me.

Grandma had once given me a box with different shaped holes and different shaped pieces to post into it, and like all my toys it had been passed on to Jed. She asked if I remembered it. "Jed can't be pushed through the rectangular hole, Bea, because he's star-shaped. And it's hard when everyone tries to squish you into the wrong shape. It's painful."

I wanted to object that I was a star too but she pulled me onto her lap and I could smell her lavender scent. Then she told me how she knew. "Granddad was a different shape too, and at his school no one said it was a lovely, interesting shape to be. They just knocked him around until all the points of his star had been broken off. They shoved him through the wrong hole so that he landed with the others. And he's still got the bruises inside."

I was shocked. Jed was always bruised on the outside and didn't seem to notice, but Granddad? I wanted to kiss him better – but I knew Grandma must have tried that.

"That was the olden days. My teachers are kind," I assured her. Then I remembered what she'd asked me. "I'll help Jed with his phonics but he'll have to sit still."

Even kind teachers were keen on that.

For a while he managed to stay whole. I suppose in Nursery and Reception there's a bounce allowance and when Jed checked in he was only just over the limit. There's an expiry date, though, and he exceeded it. When our routes around school intersected I'd hear his name, always with an exclamation mark, because straight, silent lines were hard for him to hold. The walls lured him with their artwork, and his legs preferred any and every way of travelling to the vertical, straight and steady. Sometimes when I saw his head bob up above the others, his body sway or his feet tap dance softly, I widened my eyes in warning. I even gave him a walking lesson at home but it lasted all of half a minute before he threw himself at the sofa in an attempt at a headstand.

Naturally I didn't see him in the classroom, but in Assembly I'd watch from a few rows back as his head beat a rhythm and his bottom joined in – which might have been overlooked if he'd been under the influence of Mozart or Adele, but not when the Head was talking about behaviour policy. More than once I saw him obliged to move across and sit at a teacher's feet, but it made no difference to Jed. Shoe laces were just as much fun to flick, knuckles and knees still cried out to be knocked, and the teacher who'd moved him might find her shoes stroked or the hem of her skirt rubbing his cheeks. To look at him you would have thought, as he jiggled his little backside, that it sat on a heated hob rather than a dusty school floor. I didn't know what he was thinking but I knew his body wasn't the only part of him on overdrive. Jed's imagination teemed full-time.

Did he have friends? Well, yes and no. Yes because he was only gently boisterous and never called anybody anything ruder than a burbleprobe or a lunk. No because he was exhausting and it was hard to keep pace

32

with him, physically or creatively. And because the mums witnessed the way he careered around with his school bag in the playground – probably trying to use it as a jet pack for lift-off – they tended to miss him off the party lists. Sometimes I heard Mum and Dad talk sadly about a different school, or special help, but I told them Jed was "brainy really, just not normal-clever like me." And he didn't seem unhappy because his life was so full of his own excitement, the kind everyone else missed.

It was Granddad's idea to get him a puppy. Rubadub was a floppy blond Labrador who belonged to all of us but he arrived on Jed's birthday and Jed chose his name. I loved him too – everyone did, even people in the street – but Jed was his soulmate. I wasn't jealous when he snuggled up under the duvet beside his favourite person, because I'd developed ideas about hygiene and hairs. A lot of my life was separate from Jed's now, although he went to the same Ballet and Modern classes until Madame Julie told Mum she was afraid he was too much of a handful and besides he wouldn't pass any exams if he couldn't learn the steps.

"I've got my own though," he said, showing us.

"Teach Granddad," I suggested.

There was a Christmas when Jed and Granddad performed their own version of the Nutcracker – "jangle-spangle style" – with Rubadub trying to join in. It was on two levels thanks to the coffee table, with kinds of jumping and some cushion throwing, and at one point Jed balanced on his stomach across Granddad's back and pretended to swim. I wish someone had thought to film it on a phone. I wouldn't have wanted my friends to see but I cried with laughter. And for the first time ever, I decided that my jangle-spangle brother was way too awesome for any ordinary old hole.

It was the last Christmas with Granddad on two legs or four. He had a stroke none of us could have imagined and his face shifted off-balance but the greatest loss was inside. We all tried to find the boy he'd been, Jed and Rubadub hardest of all, but there were no more space athletics, just a lot of space nothing could fill. A lot of time felt stiff with emptiness in spite of the stories we read him, and the plays Jed tried to act, none of which he seemed to understand. I told Jed his eyes were trying to do the smiling for the mouth that couldn't lift, but sometimes the shine felt like sadness instead.

People can live like that for years; I know that now. But the jangle-spangle Jed didn't survive. The boy who took his place was compliant and oddly still. I know tests could make him cry, mostly when Rubadub was the only witness. When you're a big sister you can hear crying even if it's the silent kind. He learned to hold back the answers the assessors would never think of, not in a million years. But he had trouble finding the ones they expected.

"He is a little over-sensitive at times," wrote his teacher, "and often slow to process, but I'm pleased to report that Jed has matured into a very sensible young man."

I'm at university now. Granddad's buried in a wood and I know Jed and Rubadub walk there often. Mum and Dad don't expect A or B grades at GCSE, in spite of all the studying and the worry I read in his face.

"Any ideas about the future?" I ask.

"Not really," he says.

I know he loves me almost as much as the dozy old dog, but I miss them both – Granddad Ben and Jed too. And I want my brother back.

More about *Lost Boys*

I don't suppose I would have written this story if I hadn't been a primary school teacher (for nineteen years). Now as an author I'm booked by many schools and see children like Jed because they're very visible and often audible too. My most-liked and widely-shared blogs have been about education; my YA novel *Shutdown* grew from fears about the direction it's been taking for some time, and in *The Troglin* (which backs *Alas and Alack* in the double flip-over children's book) I create in Nathan a boy whose fingers won't be still but express his imagination. Teachers are such dedicated people and now work ludicrously hard under enormous pressure. I remember one telling me that the time they want to take, as human beings, to meet the individual needs of the small humans in their care, is eaten up by the data and endless curriculum demands. I suppose my story is a reminder of diversity and individuality. As a woman with alopecia I often speak about our right to be accepted as we are without trying – and perhaps failing – to conform to society's or the media's expectations.

The story also explores the relationship between children and grandparents. We all talk about certain gifts or conditions missing a generation; for many of us that bond is very strong. This is a story of history repeating itself, but as with a bigger, global context, we need to learn better.

THE MINIMALIST

Sparse, sharp writing conceals a depth of emotion in this character's story. Geoff's well-worn path is suddenly diverted by someone with light and life and colour. The Minimalist *is a reminder that a little sentimentality is good for our souls.*

Jo Cotterill, Oxfordshire, UK, Award-winning author of many books for young people including *A Library of Lemons, Electrigirl* and *Looking at the Stars*

Rarely have I seen the experience of the blue-collar author and creative writing teacher so authentically portrayed, in a backdrop to a character study that is at once tragic and uplifting. Once more, Sue catches the human condition in a teardrop, her writing deft, deep and rich. She can say more about life in a single short story than most can manage in a novel.

Stephen Carver, Norwich, UK, Head of Online Courses at the Unthank School of Writing, reader/mentor for The Literary Consultancy, freelance editor, and cultural historian, Author of *Shark Alley: The Memoirs of a Penny-a-Liner*

What an ending. Living characters merged perfectly, lyrically, sparsely. I want the novel but the short story is perfect for this man. It's about what we miss when we over-control our experience and stick to what worked once. Life in blinkers.

Tania Clarke, Psychotherapist and coach, Herts, UK

What Sue captures so well is the uncertainty of the writer – will we ever write again, and can we ever write what truly matters – in this story of Geoff's love for his wife. Both these issues chimed with me. Read and enjoy.

Ruth Brandt, Creative Writing tutor, Surrey Adult Learning

The Minimalist *is a short story enclosing a multiplicity of short narratives, from little word portraits to a foreshortening of life. Sue plays with the format of a short story, in which the ending becomes a vignette of its own, and Geoff steps out of the frame into his own life.*

Serena Cant, Historian and Fellow of the Society of Antiquaries, Bristol, UK

THE MINIMALIST

Geoff was a minimalist. He swore by it. No tricks, nothing arsy or flash. Never overdo it. Let the silence speak, keep the sentences short and simple and remember semi-colons are for show-offs.

Having taught Creative Writing for Beginners for nine years, Geoff didn't need lesson plans or notes. He just rolled up. And so did the students, more or less regular and more or less talented. Not all of them fun, and some of them vacant. There was the occasional strop among the know-alls but he chopped them down to size along with their prose. Cutting always paid off. Apart from anything else it showed who was boss. The power of the line right through could feel quite savage and a red biro drew blood. *Padding,* he'd scrawl as justification. *Lose the flounce.*

Pace was for stepping up and rhythm must be sharp. *Too slack,* he'd slam them when they laboured it. *Needs tightening.* "One thing you must never be," he'd tell them, "is flowery." And he never was. No diversions, no excess to requirements. That way he always finished by nine thirty and there was plenty of time for the students to buy him a beer. Each, if he was lucky.

Most of them were bored out of their brains in office jobs or retail. That meant they had mental energy for an evening class, and for scribbling in between. Either they hadn't been to university or they'd done something career-driven like Business Studies or Event Management. Either way, writing was a break-out. Whether or not they crunched numbers, it was the other side of the coin – like it was for Geoff himself. But he didn't drop in personal details, and he hoped that if he did, one of them would wave a red pen in his face.

Geoff was a late starter. He'd been a Geography student at Teacher Training College, mainly for the field trips. Marrying Kath, one of the more physical girls on the course, led to job sharing as teachers to split the parenting. And no time, no energy for imagination. So now he understood the students' dreams and frustrations. The gaze to the hills.

Tarker Prize Winner, it said on his credits. That was sixteen years back but it was enough. He still used the story because he wasn't sure he'd written anything better. And introducing it that way was a kind of armour. They didn't dare question the leanness, the one-syllable choices. Since, he'd been trying to find the same edge but it always felt flabby. "I'm a one-hit wonder," he'd told Kath, long before the first cancer. "Ah, you can't beat *Na Na Hey Hey Kiss Him Goodbye*," she said, starting to sing. "But who sang it?" he demanded, and cried, "See!" as she opened her hands. He didn't want to be forgotten, and now he guessed neither did she.

"No need to stop," she said, when he said he could quit the classes. "Keep up the routine. It helps."

Routine was all it was now, he thought, as he swung off his bike outside the Sixth Form College and flattened some of the fag ends littering the drive. The leaves were always yellow by the time the course started, but they weren't falling yet. He realised he was like an actor in a show that went on year after year. Not only the same sets as backdrop but the same rise and fall in his lines, same pauses, jokes and homework. Would he still be mouthing the same lines after she'd gone?

Thirteen on the list. They wouldn't all last. Approaching the room – D7, same as last year – he heard voices. Laughter. A cocky lot? He didn't want a repeat of Karl, the Philosophy Ph.D student from 06 who thought a poetic stream of consciousness "stirred the deeply dormant" in the reader. Geoff had to break it to Karl that the only thing stirred up by such pretentious crap was the desire to jump off the nearest motorway bridge. But Karl was the fall guy still standing at Christmas. No matter how hard Geoff slapped him down, with Carver, with Hemingway or cheap one-liners, Karl came back lyrical. Geoff hoped life had drained the poesy out of him.

He was thinking that he was getting too old for kangaroo boxing when the noise from the classroom swelled. He walked in and found them relaxed, a colourful mob. The room smelt of something familiar – English lavender, like his old Suffolk gran. He realised there were ten women to two rather dingy guys, which smashed records. The younger man couldn't be more dishevelled if he'd dossed in the college through the summer, and his flaring eyes looked coked-up. The older guy, who wore a large-size suit, was tapping at his sliver of a laptop as if this was a high-street bank and someone might want to make a deposit. Geoff felt off-balance. It was like walking into a cult movie where weird is the key but nothing unlocks.

Autopilot was best. He greeted them unfazed and stood at the desk longer than usual to establish authority. The women broke off their conversations, in a reluctant and staggered way. As they settled Geoff noticed that the lavender was thickest where the colours were most Tahitian. The full-bodied black woman with a mass of black beaded hair parted her lips as if she might laugh at him.

"All right," he said, "O.K."

He went into the usual spiel about his aim to get the names right by next summer. But he wasn't going to forget Devon of the silent laugh and chinking hair, cokehead Trey or laptop Leyland. They could be escapees from the American fiction that made him want to leave Twitter. The rest of the women would keep him spinning with names like Austen girls.

Devon laughed at his first muddle. A laugh like hers was a stone in a pool. The ripples filled the room. "O.K," he said, "to business."

Devon raised her hand, and waved it too. "Can I just say something about why I'm here? Because I hate the way we all crowd like airheads around some processed pap that's meant to be sexy when the singer can't sing and the writer can't write, the TV show's a repeat in disguise and the movie's a computer-generated product spawned by marketing gurus who can't spell 'creative'. It's all a corporate capitalist con and it's empty. And I feel empty enough when I leave work because reality hurts. I want words to find meaning." The silence was anything but empty. "Not business."

Trey coughed. It was the globular kind. One of the Austens clapped and others joined in. Leyland said, "In fact I write crime fiction and was hoping for advice on getting published." The women stared. Geoff heard himself sigh. Didn't these people read what it said on the tin?

"My advice on getting published is two words. Forget it. As for meaning, you might want to try God or Nietzsche. This is a creative writing class. Feel free to leave in search of anything else and good luck."

It sounded heavier than he planned. One of the Austens, a thin woman with short hair and greying legs, bundled up her bags, muttered, "Sorry," and left. Devon ran after her.

"Well," he said, "that's cleared the air."

He'd only just got started when Devon waded back in and a couple of the Austens clapped, even though she was alone.

"She thought it was flower arranging. I told her it is, in a way. If words

40

could be flowers … whoah." Cue smile, extra-dreamy. Murmurs of ecstasy from the Austens.

Geoff thought he'd keep the *avoiding the floral at all costs* bit of the script for later. No applause for him as yet. He wondered what Kath was watching on the TV. But maybe she was in bed already. With the chemo her stamina tended to go the same way as her hair. Which was probably what Devon meant by reality. Class had never felt so far from it.

He got through to nine thirty with no rebellion. They submitted to the exercise and he didn't totally disagree when Devon's attempt earned the biggest response. "A bit of judicious paring down would work wonders," he said, taking his red pen to some of her adjectives and one pretty image. It was all in the reading. After all these years he knew how to deliver each 'before' as a limp Victorian reverie, and the 'after' like a shot of espresso.

She looked wounded but he was used to that. No one walked. The vocabulary was meant to keep them under, of course. The techniques could intimidate. The Austens made a lot of notes between them and Leyland's fingers played enough chords on his mini keyboard for a Chopin Mazurka. Devon focused, mostly straight-faced. Maybe her phone was recording every word.

"So," he ended, "no clutter, no theatre, no bouquets. Keep it real." He did the paper shuffle, the way they used to end News at Ten. "The pub over the road serves excellent beer if anyone wants to join me."

What would tempt the Austens and did he want to try? "You have a drink or two afterwards," Kath had said. "No point in rushing back."

The guys were up for alcohol but Geoff hoped Trey didn't expect him to pay. Devon persuaded one of the Asian Austens called Maria but the rest fled. Geoff felt like a manager relieved to have scraped a draw after plenty of enemy action near the goal. Stepping into the unchanged red and gold of the Royal Oak reassured him, until he saw a new face behind the bar. Two new faces and no sign of Lynda or Ky.

"We're under new management," said the youth in black with an overhang of a gelled quiff. "Refurb starts next month."

"I want the world to stop still now and then," said Devon, and he mumbled, "Yeah."

That would keep Kath sick, but alive. So really he'd rather go back, have a second shot and be a better husband. Write something worth the ink cartridge. Eat properly and wear smaller trousers. Talk more about real people and less about the Tories.

The five of them sat around the fire that used to be logs, sparks, flames and ash. Now it had a fake plastic glow. Devon was asking people about their jobs, families and 'passions' so Geoff watched the heat that pretended to flicker but just looked like a power cut was on the way. He was good at half-listening, the right faces and a few noises. He could forgive Leyland for having no passions but not for being in hedge funds. It was shaming that Trey worked for a charity. He had to buy Maria Austen a drink for being a librarian, and make a Tory bastards speech about closures which had Leyland looking shifty.

Then Devon said she must go, and Maria rose too.

"You haven't told us about yourself, Devon," said Trey.

"Oh, too many passions to list. Life and hope, as opposed to dying and indifference, you know? Way too much of it about – needs serious cutting. Music with guts and art with soul. And roses any time, but especially when they're brave and tender with frost. Oh, and poetry that sings like the earth in space." She smiled, full-on. "You probably need to take your red pen to that lot, Geoff. See you next week."

"Not necessarily," muttered Leyland.

The colour and scent faded after her. Now the guys looked sepia.

"She's great," said Trey, searching for a pen. "Poetry that sings like the earth in space." He scribbled on a beer mat and slipped it in his shirt pocket. "I've got a whale song C.D."

"Mm," said Geoff.

Rain niggled at Geoff as he pedalled home. Too many words kept revolving: not business, God or Nietzsche, if words could be flowers, too many passions to list, poetry singing like the sodding earth in bleeding space. Stray words off-script, all of them. Didn't frosted roses die, wasted? He might object less if he were more wasted himself.

The road shone like jet under headlights. The moon was timid. Adverbs killed things. Life as opposed to death. Geoff thought he should be used to the fear. No new words for it, just a stranglehold, a drum for a heart. He must fix the loose stone's tilt a step from the door.

If he was quiet she didn't wake. He padded in, poured a glass of water and took the stairs slowly.

"I'm awake," she called. Her voice could be twenty still.

He opened the door and found her in the darkness, eyes first. Sitting on his empty side of the bed, he leaned to kiss her mouth. Sexless would be the word. Her lips were cool and dry.

"Is it bad?" he asked. Words of a kind, keeping it simple.

"Mm. A bit nauseous."

"Pain?"

"Yes." He knew what that meant. He put his arms round her. "You're cold," she said. "Tell me about the new students."

So he started, undressing but not bothering to comb his hair. It was more fun in the telling than the being, and she cried, "No!" and "Really?" and "You're kidding," in between chuckles. Sliding down beside her, he kept the satire level high. Even through his ridicule, she was motherly about Trey, and told him to learn every Austen name by the end of session two. When it came to Devon, she said, "Yo!" which took him by surprise. "You've met your match at last!"

"You think so?" He was playful, muscling up above the duvet without the muscles. "That dame ain't seen the last of my red pen."

He felt tired now but she seemed wide awake. He stroked the wiry red-blond fronds from her forehead. He was a late developer when it came to such things.

"I like it when you talk to me," she said. "Tell me everything."

"About the class? You've had the extended version – with all the tutor's secret crises."

"No, the story of us. Not making fun, just straight. How we met. What you liked about me …"

She was scaring him. The words were caught in the stranglehold. "It's a very long story."

"Episode One then." She took his hand.

For just a moment he didn't think he could do it. Exhaustion closed in. Death was lying in wait and he couldn't fight it off with narrative.

"Kath was the most beautiful girl in the world …"

She elbowed him. "No embroidering! Honestly, anyone would think I was dying." He recognised the laugh even before it broke out, loose but muted too.

"Oy, behave!" he protested. If she hadn't been so frail he would have dug a playful elbow in, or kicked her foot. *"It's a love story,"* he thought.

He kissed her lightly. He was afraid now of desire and besides, how could he tell it from the rest, just as urgent, just as wild? She turned over and he waited.

"Are you sleepy now?" he whispered.

"Mm. Tell me tomorrow."

For a while Geoff lay frightened to wake her. He wasn't going to sleep. His head was still full of lavender and colour and he felt vaguely ashamed of something. But most of all he wanted to write. In his head he was wording who his wife had been, who she was and had become. Remembering the days when he'd kept a notebook by the bed, he couldn't think why he'd stopped. But he mustn't disturb her. He eased out from under the duvet, avoiding the creak and breathing in an expletive when he knocked his calf against the bed frame. He slipped into his dressing gown and made his way carefully downstairs.

It was a sick joke that he'd only just thought to begin. In the study he turned on the old P.C., telling his brain to wait. No need for a tumbling splurge. They might have a few months yet. But then the slowness of the start seemed outrageous because however long the dying took it would be too fast. Against the darkness, the curtains looked blotchy. A wind wiped a trace of branches behind them. Was that a stain he'd forgotten on the carpet, or a shadow?

At last the screen was blank, the cursor flashing.

For Kath

I was a shambles at nineteen. You had a sense of self before I knew there was any such thing. I remember your bell bottoms and cheesecloth shirts and what you called desert boots. You always looked ready for a field trip, even at a bop in the SU Hall. Except then you added a choker and lipstick. I don't dare guess the date we started going out because you'll have it stored in your head like everyone's birthdays and anniversaries. But I remember the first kiss.

Geoff sighed. It had been cleared by the millions after it, or some composite best-of version. No one could write love scenes anyway. The spare ones were brutal and the others were a con. He deleted the last sentence because she wanted honesty, always had.

'Genuine', Mum called you. It runs right through. We were like an old married couple by the time we graduated, except we shagged our way through everything. It's

the only way to get through Teaching Practice sober, you said. Hussy. The skinny dipping in Ullswater on that second field trip was our mad secret even though I wanted to brag about loving you against a new dawn sky. Your red hair turned dark and sleek and the water was cold as hell.

Geoff looked at the screen. Who was this for? No straining for effect. There'd be no book deal. Only for her. And wouldn't that make her cry, and long for a past that didn't warn them?

I still don't know why you chose me. God knows I was a goon, all limbs and centre parting. We were a pair of magnets. Clunk. Till death did them part.

If he could erase the 09 student with the come-on mouth and come-on tears … It was just a sloppy fumble but all the more tawdry for that. And then he'd had to harden so cold in class that she quit. Did Kath guess? At the time he'd thought she might. Guilt had stalked him, followed them around and joined them in bed. Kath could have done so much better.

I was proud that you skipped bridal white, and told your dad you weren't his to give. Such a well-mannered rebel. She wouldn't be using his name if hers hadn't been Windsor. A republican Socialist and she'd got past his parents with smiles and kindness. Soon they loved her more than him. She'd talk on the phone for ten minutes, fifteen, before she'd say, "Geoff, it's your mum."

Geoff heard a sound upstairs. He saved what he'd written under *Kath* and shut down. She was in the bathroom, the door ajar.

"Kath? You all right?"

"Fine."

He waited for her to emerge. Her hair was thin now, thinner each day, but still trying to be frenzied. It was too fragile to touch but it had its own feel, a spring and a roughness against his cheek as he held her.

"What's wrong?" she asked. "What were you doing down there?"

"Writing."

She was jubilant. "Great! Write like you've got one more day."

If there's one thing more ridiculous than your courage, it's your faith in me.

He ran a glass of water for her painkillers and watched her swallow. A vase stood upside down on the draining board; her sister's peeling roses had been relegated to the bin.

"You really love flowers, don't you?"
She smiled and nodded. He'd buy more tomorrow.

More about *the Minimalist*

Those who have studied Creative Writing will know the impact of Raymond Carver, held up for some years now as the model for a style that's lean and mean. Some won't have heard that it was his editor Gordon Lish who cut his short story manuscripts without his permission, making many changes to names, character, plot, mood and ending. Carver's original wasn't lean or mean! It was the edited collection, *What We Talk About When We Talk About Love,* that won awards, but since the original was published as *Beginners*, critical opinion has been divided about which is greatest. It's a true story that teaches us a lot about the book world.

My character Geoff is a Carver fan in a story that's satirical until his world reshapes itself and his rules begin to change. It explores the way the word *flowery* is used to condemn writing on the grounds of excessive description or feeling, but also the emotional importance of flowers as gifts in our lives. Like poetry they're for celebration and consolation – and perhaps it's the poetry in prose that Geoff rejects, but haven't symbols been powerful through history? Hasn't beauty?

What makes great writing? Answers on a postcard! I must hesitate to add that although Leslie Tate and I have been booked by many writers' groups to talk about our work, Geoff and the members of his class have been imagined rather than lifted from any particular visit!

AUDITION

This is a brave piece. Every time I write something political, half my friends tell me I'm telling them what to think (oddly they never say this when I write about love or loss or anything else human). I didn't feel you were telling me what to think about poverty or Aleppo, though I know what you think about them. I really liked the angel audition device that holds these themes in place. Stories may not save us, but they do give us materials to think and feel with. Thank you.

Neil McDonald, Surrey, UK,
Author of stories published in Structo, Gold Dust and other journals

An uplifting, ethereal tale of dark circumstance, Audition *is very powerful, very Zeitgeist and wonderfully Sue Hampton.*

Tracey West, Dorset, UK,
Author of *Poetry of Divorce* and *Diary of Divorce* pub Magic Oxygen

It would have been very easy to take the premise of this story and write something overly florid or twee, but Sue Hampton has somehow managed to produce an engagingly matter-of-fact account of extraordinary events. Guy, a young actor whose beautiful hair isn't enough to win him much work, attends an audition and finds himself giving the performance of his life in a role which he inhabits almost immediately. This isn't easy material, but it has been wrought by capable hands.

Nicky Coates, Singer-songwriter, Bristol, UK

AUDITION

It was just another job I wouldn't land. I'd become quite settled at the pizza place and had expectations close to zero.

"Yeah but you look the part, right?" said Mitch. "No point me going for it."

Mitch is grizzled for twenty-eight. He reckons he could take the lead in *Fiddler on the Roof* and make it edgy. In the meantime, he's a mortgage adviser so the first, second and third rounds at The Crown and Anchor over the road are all on him.

"I do?" I asked, looking at myself on my phone screen.

Mitch flicked up some of the curls I pulled back in a ponytail for waiting tables. "Pre-Raphaelite or what?"

Mitch knows his art; I don't, beyond the waterlilies and the sunflowers.

"If you say so." I tapped in a search and up they came, in stained glass. "Like a girl, you mean."

"Yeah, Guy, you got it."

I've been to a few theatres where forty of us have been on stage together, dancing some routine the others picked up faster than me. This time the audition postcode meant nothing. I arrived in a mist that wouldn't lift. Had I got some digit wrong?

I was standing outside a foodbank. Not the kind they have in church halls and not much of a warehouse – more the size of a prefab classroom. A black guy emerged, holding a couple of bags in one hand and his small daughter's hand in the other. He wasn't so much older than me but I read the despair that lowered his shoulders and kept his eyes ahead. I wondered how much the child understood, and how hard it must be for her father to make sure she knew nothing about hunger, debt, crap housing, fear ...

I would have walked away but I'd spent two hours' wages on

conditioner.

"Come on in." The voice was female. Not sexy like a proposition, but not bossy P.M. either. It was clear blue, no clouds.

There was a side door with the word CASTING taped to it. I pushed it open and found a row of plastic chairs, three of them occupied. The hopefuls waiting their turns were good-looking lads but between them they couldn't match my hair. Then I remembered the mist and checked for damage. It had shrunk and clung a bit. Would they see the potential?

"All right?" I said, but they were in the zone.

A door opened and a solid, heavy-breasted girl with punky hair and piercings looked directly at me. "Guy," she said. "Follow me."

The corridor seemed long so as we walked I asked her name. "Sky," she told me, with a freckled grin that was very young. "You'd be my choice but I'm not picking."

I was about to ask who was in charge of that when she opened a door on a dark, Middle-Eastern woman behind a desk. Her skin glowed and her eyes were beautiful but she was mature and substantial.

"Guy," she said. "Welcome. It's good of you to volunteer."

"Uh ... I came for a job, right?"

"A rewarding one," she said, "in its own way. What makes you think you'd be convincing in this role?" She smiled brightly. "That's aside from what the mirror tells you."

"Well ..."

"Would you say there's a crying need for more of them, out in the real world?"

"For sure. But are we talking stage or film?"

She smiled again and I wished she was my mother. "Your hands, Guy. May I touch?"

I must have known by this point that the weirdness dial had spun to max but I laid my hands on the desk in front of her. The nicotine stains had cleared since I quit but I couldn't guarantee there was no trace of garlic in my fingernails. Her own fingers rested briefly on mine as she turned my palms up, and lifted one onto her shoulder. I felt the firmness of her bones and the warmth of her.

"Believe," she said, and waited. "Is your conviction absolute?"

"Sure," I told her. Something in me had shifted and I didn't care about anything but playing the part. I felt as if I'd already begun.

She let my hand go. Now it felt light and clean and hardly mine. "You haven't lived an easy life."

I tried to remember what I'd put on the application form. Only previous roles, surely? Education, such as it was. But I could tell she knew exactly what she meant.

"That gives me insight," I said, clouding. I didn't bother to wipe the trickle as it ran down my left cheek. She nodded, leaned forward and reached to stroke it away.

"My turn to believe," she said. Standing, she closed her hands and said. "Congratulations, and welcome."

I'm not sure which of us began the hug. She smelt like a festival: sweet, floral and spiced. If she'd told me she was my mother, back to hold me, I would have bought it. Then she handed me an envelope, fat with cash.

"Expenses," she said.

"I walked most of the way …"

"You'll need it."

"Thank you," I said as I left.

"Namaste," I heard behind me.

Outside, sun had transformed the industrial estate. Leaves glistened. Stepping out, I felt disorientated, as if I'd just woken from a nap I shouldn't have taken. I had to think hard about my route home.

Glancing at the foodbank exit I saw a girl younger than me: hair thin and straggly, body mass index too low, heels too high for purpose. She had a baby in an old buggy with a wheel that stuck like supermarket trolleys try to do. A bag hanging from a handle made it tip a bit as she struggled to kick the wheel into line with one boot.

"Hey," I said. "Need a hand?"

The way she looked at me, I thought she might tell me to fuck off but she was just weighing me up. I didn't blame her. I unlocked the stuck wheel with my foot and thought of offering to carry the bag of food but she'd think I planned to run off with it. So I just smiled at the baby, and asked how old 'it' was.

"He's seven months," she said. "Starting to roll when my back's turned."

He was sleeping with a bubble of dribble between his lips. We started walking and I held back the questions that weren't my business.

"Thanks then," she said, which meant I didn't need to stick around.

"You hungry? Can I get you lunch? I'm not a pimp or anything and I'm not trying to get in your knickers."

She turned to me, her eyes narrowing with doubt. "Why then?"

"I'm an actor," I said. "I've got work so I'm celebrating. It's a kind of rehearsal for a new role."

"What role?"

"Well, I know a place that does ham, or cheese, or even chicken salad."

"Be secretive then."

"You won't see me on *EastEnders*," I told her.

"Go on then," she said. "Thanks."

She fancied fish and chips and that was fine by me. We sat down in a place that tried to be a cool American-style diner but didn't pull it off. It turned out Shelley had missed her tea for a few days since she'd run right out of most things, so now she made up for it with three milky mugs. Sometimes, she said, when she couldn't afford to heat food, she ate baked beans or meatballs cold from the tin.

"You're a good listener," she said. There was salt on her top lip. "I guess actors have to be."

She asked about me but I don't talk about the darkness. There are things it's not fair to share. Zac woke and took centre stage then anyway. He had her eyes but a lot more flesh on him. He reached up but I told her to clear her plate and managed to unclip him. He started playing with my hair and I remembered about jiggling and big bright eyes and mouths. I turned it on, playing the perfect dad – and got a bit carried away nose to nose. Zac loved the performance. My best ever critic.

Shelley had popped her last chip by this point so I handed him over and I could see he wanted food too.

"I'm going to flash my tits now but don't get any ideas," she said, unbuttoning.

"All right," I said. "I'll pay and leave you to it."

"No need to go. You seen nips before, right?"

"I'd best be going," I said.

Remembering the director's brief I laid a hand on her shoulder just a moment. Any longer and she would have spun away and thrown Zac off too. I paid for the meals and then, on my way out, I gave her some money. I didn't count it, just took a few twenties out and gave her the envelope, writing my number on it.

"You could call me if you needed to. I'm not much of a plumber or electrician but I know people. Wannabe actors don't all wait tables."

I was expecting a *"What the fuck?"* but she didn't say a word. She didn't open the envelope either. She just sat there with Zac on her breast and her eyes shining.

"Take care, you two," I said, and walked away. In my head I heard Mitch: *"You did what?"* but I felt warm, salty and full and strangely calm.

I was an angel now.

For a while I just walked, rerunning everything: the audition like no other, the girl and her baby. The role, and how I was already easing into it. I couldn't imagine how to tell Mitch, who's a practical guy, shrewd, careful. *"And you don't even know how much you gave her?"* We're opposites in some ways and that's how it works; this time it's really love – even though Mitch might joke, *"Who says for me it's not pure lust?"* He's gentle in his way, and not just with the cat, but I knew he wouldn't understand.

I'd probably missed a load of opportunities by the time I shook myself out of my own incredulous inner narrative and used my senses. I needed to be alert. *Desolation Row*, Dad used to sing when he was pissed. It was everywhere but I had to detect isolation beyond basic loneliness. Approaching a crossing I saw an old man in a Parka and grubby trainers, bending and squinting towards the traffic. I stood beside him, closer than I needed to, and he shuffled aside as if he thought I might mug him.

"All right?" I asked.

He didn't answer and I wasn't sure whether deafness stopped him, or language, or fear. He gave me a suspicious glance or two before the lights changed. He was slow but mobile and wouldn't want an arm to hold. So all I did was take my time alongside him. Then when we'd crossed, I gave him a smile.

"Have you got shopping to do? Need some help carrying it?"

He stared and his frown was almost fierce. So many lines in one face. Then a woman with a Yorkshire Terrier passed by. The little dog was perky and pert and glad to be alive. He grinned after it, then looked back at me.

"Not a lot of shopping when you're on your own, lad," he said. "Got bills to pay."

"Sure," I said. "Well, if you ever need company or help, totally free of charge …" I'd have to get some cards printed at this rate, with wings in the logo. I wrote my phone number on the back of a bus ticket. "I'm Guy."

He was all grooved skin and dark eyes again now. "What's the catch then? Scams they call them. What's your game, Guy?"

A pigeon landed at his feet and I expected him to shoo or even kick it but he felt in his pocket and found a few thin crumbs to scatter. Then he reached out and took the ticket I was holding out, looking dumbly at the last few notes from my expenses before he took those too.

"Help with that bill?" I suggested.

"You know my name," he said.

I was slow to process that. He held out a hand for me to shake and when I pulled mine away I rested it a moment on his arm.

"Good to meet you, Bill," I said.

He nodded and I could see that whatever he was thinking about was bigger than the weather or the traffic. He headed towards the station with a lift of one hand and I wondered whether I'd see him again, because I'd be sad not to. Shelley and Zac too.

Still, I needed to get my bearings. This job was messing with gravity; I was lighter now. But I was weary too, and when I saw my reflection in a shop front I stopped to scrutinise what I saw, to check off the features and reassure myself who I was. A pretty gay dude with not much going for me but a role I could make my own, as they say — because it's all pretending anyway: all red velvet, costume and clever lighting. But not grubby streets alive with litter caught by wind, graffiti and dog shit that nobody cared enough to scoop up.

I didn't tell Mitch I got the job because I didn't know how. Instead I was vague, as if I was waiting to hear. I cooked him a supper I knew he'd like, from a cookery book we hadn't opened since Christmas, and told him I love him because as a species we don't do that enough.

"Are you all right, Guy?" he asked me, looking inside the way he does when he stops joking about and gets sensitive.

We were on the sofa after supper, clothed but connected.

"I'm happy," I said, even though I'd only just realised.

In spite of the crap day he'd had at work, trying to talk to someone at Head Office about links with the arms trade, that made him happy too.

"You think I'm the provider," he said, "the solid one. But you save me."

I told him he must be drunk again.

That night I must have dreamed. Not the usual incoherent fantasy adventures, not Dad shouting and shoving, and not Mum on the motorway bridge – or at the foot of it either. No roadkill but there was blood all right. It was bright in the ash-grey dust. Above our heads planes no bigger than black gulls swept by. Then they were lost in swelling fire, bitter and black. Screams, groans, shouts, sobbing bombarded us. Like ants on a hot tile, people ran with no direction. There was a cart, bare metal and slow, loaded with children and pushed by fathers. A mother carried a baby to her chest, arms crossed like a stone figure on a tomb.

I knew this was East Aleppo. I have a Facebook account. There was blood on my hands and when I wiped it on my jeans it only smeared red as ever. I didn't know whether or where I hurt but my heart was an animal inside me, clawing to be free.

As the wind caught the dust, the stone that used to be whole fragmented, whirling in smoke. It was hard to see. Among the cries I heard a noise that might have broken from inside me, because my lungs were torn and burning and my breath was gritty and dark, but I knew it was a child.

It was a shoe I saw first, an open-toed purple 'jelly'. Not much leg with it. I'm no Paramedic but I crouched down and reached in. To start with, I only touched the skin above the ankle, resting to reassure.

"O.K.," I said, because that's universal, right?

From inside the torn concrete I heard the crying mute. Carefully I cleared the rubble, talking all the time, until the words I spoke had no meaning, or just one. The child's arms opened, mine too, and the clinging was on both sides. Boy or girl, I couldn't tell. Age? Maybe six. The flesh felt hot, damp, light over bone. Looking all around me I turned, three hundred and sixty degrees, more, not knowing what I hoped to see. A bright shiny hospital in one piece? A team wearing white helmets?

I knew the word hurled towards me was a name because the body in my arms tensed and stretched towards it. Now a man was running towards me, his eyes livid through the grey, shouting the syllables again and again. His jagged voice snapped and rebuilt again. The child cried out too. I passed him or her into the father's care, and I guessed the word that tumbled out next meant thank you. Standing free, I remembered. I placed a hand on the man's shoulder. Then they were gone.

Turning back to the wreckage I wondered who else might be lying beneath its weight. "Hello?" I yelled, climbing. I heard a cat, and eased it free but limping. Then an old woman, one elbow twisted, one leg gashed. As I laid a hand on her shoulder I felt whole and strong. Time was different now, fluid, cloudy.

I don't suppose anyone ever knows what happened. One moment I was tall and scrambling. Then I was on the ground and the taste was bitter but I couldn't spit. Not now. Heat melted me. Light shrouded me.

Now I'm in demand, more than ever. Rehearsals are over; the role became full-time. I'm around for Shelley, watching out for Zac. I hope Mitch knows I'll never leave him. And I've never felt more alive.

More about *Audition*

This is one of the shorter stories and unusually for me, ventures into the territory of magic realism. I began it with a premise and an ending and soon it was complete. Someone noted that the style is a departure for me too: shorter sentences, more urban register. I put that down to my character, Guy, because he's a young Londoner with no faith in the religious sense. His narrative voice has a realist's edge; you might call him cynical. But he begins with an experience of love and his understanding of all that it can mean quickly grows. Over two thousand words I grew to love and believe in him.

Yes, I believe in supporting refugees. I'm a Trustee for a small charity called People Not Borders and that's what we do, in a number of ways. When I wrote the story we had just been able to fill over 700 Bags of Love for children in Syrian hospitals, and as I write this introduction I've just seen a video of children in Aleppo opening the bags and smiling. We've also raised money to buy medical equipment for Syria. I don't believe in war as a solution to anything and last year I protested with CAAT (Campaign Against the Arms Trade) up at Parliament Square about the UK supplying arms to Saudi Arabia, in spite of UN concerns about their war crimes in the Yemen. And yes, I saw *I, Daniel Blake* a few weeks before I wrote the story. I went with fellow-Quakers to our nearest foodbank, and support it.

Everyone will have called someone an angel or wanted to believe they exist. They're part of our vocabulary, and artworks in all media are full of them. Hollywood has offered a few. Like John Travolta I've created an unusual angel, a product of our times, at a moment in human history when we need a whole skyful.

THE SIMLA PALACE

A really thoughtful story. Sue has definitely conveyed the often too real emotions attached to a long marriage, when children and life have taken their toll. I enjoyed Sue's interchanging perspectives, switching between husband and wife – although the story itself, about the loss of what once was, made me feel a little sad. Beautifully written, with a genuine and heartfelt insight into life inside a twenty-nine year relationship.

Michelle Briscombe, Cardiff, Wales, UK,
Author of *Silent Mountain* and *The House on March Lane*

Norma and Brian's 29 year-old marriage is in more trouble than either realises. He is stuck in his ways, Norma's tongue is getting sharper and inertia seems to be the dominant force in their dealings with the world and each other. The story is exquisitely written. Although neither character is especially likeable – Brian is irredeemable and Norma would command more sympathy if she had a little more courage – their fate is intriguing. The anniversary dinner is presented through both sets of eyes alternately, perhaps to allow both characters in turn to express themselves, but ultimately it reinforces the impression that there is very little common ground on which they can hope to meet.

David Guest, Herts, Journalist & author of *A Pressure of the Hand*

Beautifully written as always with Sue Hampton, there are some very evocative and stirring lines in The Simla Palace, *which pop out and hit home from what is a seemingly gentle narrative. It feels like regret and resentment just about remains below the surface, but Norma never manages to muster the strength or desire to break out of it in a big way.*

Lisa Emery, Reason Café and Bookshop, Herts, UK

THE SIMLA PALACE

Norma and Brian had been to The Simla Palace for their last seven or eight anniversaries, including the Silver Wedding. That year Norma had been allowing herself to imagine Paris. He'd probably had Chicken Korma and a Peshwari Nan on each *occasion* but Norma thought the word had a fanfare about it that those evenings didn't deserve. Topping up her foundation, she looked at the grooves that had been ploughed through her skin since their wedding day. That eye bag could be down to money worries – his, the infectious kind that spoiled things. And the creases on the side of her mouth, making her look like a Thunderbird brother, were probably thanks to Hayley and Jemma – and the way they used to scrap, or tug at her like two blackbirds with different ends of the same worm. Still, it was quiet without them.

She sprayed on some perfume, placed it back among the pots and tubes of creams that didn't seem to be doing their job and considered juggling a few of them, whirling them through the air just to prove she still could. Brian used to show her off. In pubs she'd toss beermats, and in coffee shops it was teaspoons. He'd laughed off the first breakage, bound to happen now and then. But now she thought his doubt set in before hers. So many things had gone the same way as the French verbs she used to *decline*. Looking back, she could see the road from crowd pleaser to health and safety liability was a short one, and maybe she'd slept through it because she didn't remember a thing about it.

The ears remained functional enough to report that Brian was still watching *Eggheads*. But she had to admit it took him all of two minutes to get ready, zap a bit of aftershave up his armpits and work a comb. He still had lovely hair, much thicker and sleeker than hers; she kept on encouraging him to grow it like a younger Rolling Stone but he said it wouldn't *go down well* at work. With retirement a few years off she wasn't sure why he hated disapproval. As far as Norma could see, being past caring what people thought of her was the one and only triumph that came with *getting on a bit* and she'd made hers worth strutting about for a while now.

"No!" she heard from downstairs.

Brian was always despairing of the ignorance of contestants, especially the young ones. He liked to think he'd stashed a lot of knowledge away over the years: dates and capitals in particular. Norma had decided that her brain was resistant to such facts. It reminded her of the old Bird's Eye advert where the big boulder of a pea couldn't get in the packet however hard it tried.

"Why do you know *that*?" he'd ask, when she was sitting there beside him and supplied the name of a Spice Girl baby or a film star's first wife.

"I can't help it," she'd say, not much of a defence. Such things stuck. Comments made by friends about their husbands' habits, in bed or out; theme tunes of sitcoms; whole scenes from Kevin Costner movies because there was a time when she'd rewind and replay his smile.

Norma pulled her good shoes out of the wardrobe and told herself she was lucky really. How many people these days managed twenty-nine years of marriage? And The Simla Palace was nice, reliable. She shouldn't be a grouch. Maybe she should give up work; she was starting to feel weary. But Brian would scoff at that and then they'd be back in the old argument about who had more to do, or put up with – him with his psycho boss at Boredom Incorporated, or her, with the bakery and the shopping, cooking and cleaning, keeping the garden in order and him and the cats too. That was what they called too close to call!

Norma decided to walk down the stairs in heels like the dancers had to on *Strictly*, taking it slowly but throwing in a bit of sway as she held on to the banister. She imagined finding Brian waiting at the bottom, watching, grinning and enjoying it – and her. In fact he was still on the sofa, even though the credits were rolling on screen.

"I don't know what the schools think they're doing," he said, switching off without looking at her. "No idea which Royal was Shakespeare's patron, I ask you!"

"Princess Diana?" suggested Norma, deadpan. "Haul your grits then."

Norma smiled, remembering using the phrase when they first starting sleeping together, and his helpless laughter – delight, really. An expression like that was what they called a blast from the past but she had no idea where it came from. Brian didn't react except with his usual, "Yeah, all right." If she'd said, *"Art thou not ready then dearest?"* or, *"Make some effing effort for an effing change!"* she'd have got the same response. He used to say she was fun. Hauling grits was part of it, like *"Better than a slap round the gizzard with a cold cod."* She reminded herself that marriage to Brian was probably that, at least.

"Two ticks," he said, as headed upstairs.

For the first time she saw feedback boxes instead of a second hand clicking round. "I'd give you one, if you're lucky," she muttered. Then she hoped he hadn't heard, in case he thought he was on a promise.

Norma collected the West Ham mug from the carpet at his end of the sofa, and took it to the kitchen sink. She should have nipped these habits in the bud but now they were in full bloom and flourishing.

"How many grits have you got to haul," she yelled, "after all these years?"

Brian knew she'd made some impatient remark or other, some wisecrack, but he'd told her enough times that the old hearing wasn't what it was, a situation he could blame on following Quo around the country through the decades. If he'd written to Rossi and Parfitt and told them so before it was too late, they'd have given him a season ticket and got him up on stage – which would have been worth more than a lawsuit, not that Norma would understand. She used to go with him until the kids came along but now she was scathing. As if she had any ear whatever for how many chords they played.

Casting a quick glance in the bathroom mirror, he wondered whether the new girl at work realised how old he was. No one would think the only exercise he ever had was sex, and that was about as regular as an England victory. Only he could produce a whole stack of figures for any public kind of scoring, no need for three options to choose from. What was she wearing tonight? He couldn't be sure. She'd kept her figure better than most but these days he had an idea people could take him for her toy boy. He could just picture the way that would make her throw back her head and let rip!

The thing about Norma, thought Brian, was that you couldn't be sure what she really meant, or what was happening on the inside when she was joking on the surface. Probably by the time those Eggheads had made all kinds of convoluted mental sweeps into the corners of their brains to try to find some fact that was hiding – like the other red sock or that one missing piece from his World Flags jigsaw – they'd be swearing furiously but silently under the smiles. But you couldn't tell, because they just calmly admitted they were afraid they didn't know, Jeremy. Norma had plenty to say all right, but half the time he could do with a translator for what you'd call the subtext.

Thirty years next time. Was that anything special, officially? He'd failed at the twenty-fifth hurdle and that was just misjudgement, but the girls reckoned he'd got some making up to do. What had Norma called him? Was it a skinflint, a bozo or a fool? All three, probably, to her friends. In The Simla Palace she'd given him the silent treatment. Not that she could keep it up. He didn't mean to disappoint her but gestures had never really been his style. He was there for her when it mattered with her dad, though: all those drives to the hospital through winter darkness and the rush hour. Grim memories, they'd aged her anyway. A silent Norma had been a painful sound.

Sometimes Brian wished the current Norma would be a bit more ... fragrant. *Which politician's wife was described in court ...?* Everyone knew that, even Norma. More lady-like. She seemed determined through the menopause to up the antis, every one of them. On a night like this, it meant less said the better – on his side, anyway.

"How did you two even get together?" Jemma asked a while back, when she visited with her dozy fella. As if it was a mystery.

Then Norma jumped in, "He can't answer stuff like that. Stick to the Periodic Table and he'll be happy as a snout in muck all afternoon."

Of course that boyfriend of Jemma's knew nothing. And Brian didn't insist it was on a Friday at the Romford Palais. Or that her hair had that scented, wet smell when he got up close because she never bothered with brollies in those days. In any case, there was a chance he could be wrong about the day or the club, or even the girl. When it came to those, he'd had more than three options to choose from.

Greeted at the restaurant door by 'the handsome one', Norma felt guilty. Shouldn't they know everybody's name by now? Brian was the one with a storage facility of a brain; he should take care of all that.

"Happy anniversary!"

"Yes, come round again," said Brian, in the same kind of voice he'd use about the tax form. He did the nodding dog head thing.

A couple more of the waiters appeared to congratulate them and they were led to their usual table, where five red roses budded in a narrow vase. Norma told the guys they were darlings, thanked them more than once and sat down with a smile, smoothing the crisply folded napkin on her lap.

"Pushed the boat out with those," muttered Brian, nodding to the roses. "Tesco special offer?"

"Not special enough to tempt you," she retorted.

"I remember you saying red roses are usually a confession." He lowered his voice even further. "Of adultery …"

He remembered all the wrong things! Norma shelved an image of the roses hurled into a spin and her last ever juggle ending in bloody debris, her fingers gushing and spraying innocent bystanders. "I'm enjoying being spoiled. Was, anyway. Must be the new manager's idea. Let's have that fizz the young people drink. Prozaccio!" She laughed. "Just what the doctor ordered."

"Prosecco," he muttered.

"I know what it's called, Brian. But they might be renaming it by the morning." She rolled her eyes. "Joke! Don't panic. You look off-colour all of a sudden."

She told herself she mustn't tease him in public; it always made him grumpy. But it wasn't every day four young men put a twinkle in her eye, with bows and smiles and roses. When was the last time she'd giggled her way through an evening with Brian? Or a whole five minutes?

She stuck with red wine; Brian had his Indian beer. The waiter asked how many years it was now and she said, "Don't ask him – he only knows important stuff like the gestation period of a camel. Twenty-nine years." She grinned. "Poor bloody camel!"

When they were alone again Brian mumbled, "Turn it down, will you?"

"Down to *off*?"

"Sorry?" Usually when he said that she knew he wasn't sorry, only cross.

"Nothing." The drinks came and she sipped her wine. "We've never had a full-blown row on our anniversary, have we?"

"I hope that's not a warning."

She'd called him Mr Sardonic, and Mr Low-Low Key. He could be Mr Serrated Edge too but that wasn't funny. Norma decided that the change of life was making her a bit wild but she wasn't going to apologise for it.

On the other hand, she'd try to be wifely because he probably couldn't help it either. And if she didn't say something soon as he looked at her over the flowers, he'd probably quiz her on Rosa family genuses: ten, ten thousand or ten billion and one.

"We've never really done top ten highlights," she said.

"Of our marriage?"

"No, Brian, of Food and Drink rounds! Let's do five between us, not counting the wedding itself, or the girls being born, or any summer holidays."

"No holidays?" Brian looked like the BBC had just announced that Kevin Ashman had left the show.

"Too obvious. Let's go for the obscure answers other people haven't thought of." Brian had made it clear often enough that he didn't think *Pointless* was serious enough for real quizzers. "My first highlight was going for walks on Sunday afternoons when we were fit and frisky and there were no pushchairs or theme parks in our lives. And we held hands."

Brian smiled. "You liked that?" He looked as if he did too. "We walked miles … and still had energy at the end."

Did he mean sex? They always remembered things differently. "But that's too far back in the mists of time," she diverted. "I mean, who can see through the rosy haze? To really score you have to find a highlight from the last nine years, not the first twenty." She threw that challenge out with a forefinger, like a bossy bat. Was she becoming one? Who was that girl who liked walking anyway?

"So from August nineteen eighty …"

"It's not maths, Brian. There's leeway."

"Right." He paused. The popadums arrived. "Is this necessary? It feels like I'm on the spot. We could just enjoy the food."

Norma felt the pull of frustration, a kind of twang that made things tight and threatened to ping back again. Perhaps he'd find it easier to roll off highlights from his free and single days. Or countries on the Equator.

"Never mind," she said. "I take it the Eggheads won? What's the jackpot up to now, twenty five million? Why don't you challenge them single-handed and pocket the lot?"

The Korma was creamy but Norma seemed to be in a funny mood. Watching the colour rise in her cheeks, Brian wondered whether the hormones were making her angry and impatient as well as edging her volume up. She used to be softer, not demure exactly but not confrontational either. It was normal, after so long, to allow for pauses in conversation. Even Norma couldn't talk non-stop for twenty-nine years! But it felt like she was counting the lengths of the silences, weighing them, and that made them harder to brush off with comments like, "Is that good?" or "They're busy tonight." So he tried, "How's Sandra?" but all he got back was, "Fine." As if he'd imagined Sandra's back problem even though he'd heard all the details of that not more than a fortnight ago.

"Malleus, incus and stapes," he said. "Are all – wait for this – opticals, ossicles or oracles! And the girl – who obviously doesn't know a lot about Ancient Greece – said ..."

"Do you want another beer? I'm going to have another glass of red."

"All right ..."

"Questions like that are just poking fun anyway."

She must know the answer though, surely? "Oh, I don't know. I wouldn't say that."

The music around them, which was usually Bollywood on mute, had changed. British Eighties New Romantics. Spandau Ballet, was it? He could probably name the line-up if he had to ...

Norma's face had changed with the song, from the bottom lip up.

"I don't think I ever told you ..." she said, girlish all of a sudden. "Ah," she said, smiling at the waiter because their starters had arrived. By the time she'd ordered the drinks the track was nearly over but she just sat and listened, with her fork over the plate. He wasn't sure but there could be something wrong.

"Told me?" he prompted.

"Never mind."

"I wouldn't have thought there could be anything you haven't told me." He smiled. Everything was a story with Norma, unless she'd run out of energy like their laughing Santa generally did long before twelfth night.

"Ah well ... here's a question for you. Three facts about Norma – but only one is true." He couldn't name the edge in her voice.

"So one fact?"

"Yes, Brian. So first option: I once rode an elephant called True. Well, in translation." She paused. "Second: I had a one-night stand after a Spandau Ballet concert. Third: I bought a coat just like the one Tony Hadley wore at Live Aid from a market stall but it had me in a muck sweat too."

"The coat," he said, confidently. She loved elephants but hated circuses. And he could imagine her, when he met her, in some such thing. Her hair was spiked up with gel in those days.

Norma shook her head. "I looked hard enough though."

One of the waiters came to ask whether everything was all right. Suddenly Brian wasn't sure.

Norma knew her face was red. She tilted the wine in her glass and wished things were different. Including her options. But whatever else she threw in with the one night stand, he'd never go for that, because men like him notched those up if they could but they didn't marry sluts. Norma remembered hearing that even Mr Darcy wouldn't have been a virgin for Lizzie Bennet. Gents like him learned a few things in some up-market brothel in Paris or Vienna.

But why the lie, now? To spice up the Korma? To make him think for once, instead of just dragging something out of his memory banks for a quick airing? To make him look at her as well as hear her? To make him use the imagination he never exercised, before the moths ate it and left a hole behind? It made no difference now because she'd started so she'd finish.

"If it's not the coat?" she prompted.

"Don't," he barked, so low the word was almost hidden.

"I'd like to think I could still surprise you. As opposed to boring you rigid – when I'm not annoying the hell out of you." She leaned across into his half of the table, her fingers dancing around the stem of the glass.

"You surprise me," he said, pulling his everything-is-under-control face. "We can talk about it at home."

Norma smothered her smile. "O.K." She chased a slippery aubergine chunk and pierced it. So he wanted to know. "Where in Kenya do most of the roses come from then?"

He couldn't resist a question like that.

66

As she held his arm up the drive, she said, "I'm tiddly as a guppy." That was a new one but he pointed out she couldn't be, or she wouldn't be able to say it. A mistake, because she repeated it, faster each time, and only stopped to escape from her shoes, showing him what they'd done to her feet where red skin swelled. It frightened him to think of Jemma and Hayley going out drinking, preloading and all that when they'd been little sweethearts and run to the door when he came home: "Daddy!" How long did that last? Not worth trying to answer. But Norma used to tell him how important consistency was, that he undermined her with her rules about food and bedtimes. If there was one thing Norma didn't like to be called it was *soft*. Because she didn't mean to be.

Soft was how she felt as he helped her with her coat.

"Steady," he said, even though she seemed perfectly stable – in a physical sense, anyway.

"I'm fine," she said. "This guppy will just swim upstairs."

Following her, he thought how well he knew her backside. That familiarity they lived with, he'd thought it went deep. All the way. There were stories he'd heard so often he could gag her and finish them in half the time. And now she threw in this episode she'd always edited out – because she was ashamed, he supposed. Or used to be. Because she didn't care about sparing him anymore?

Most people would say it didn't matter. But facts always did. Quizzers knew that. And bedroom facts were the ones they put on front pages and Home Pages, the ones they called revelations. She knew that. Had she planned it? He'd no idea why she'd held it back four years ago when he messed up, and she could have laid it on him then as a punishment to fit his crime.

From the family bathroom he heard her in the en suite, humming. That song – only for a few seconds, but did it slip out, or was it meant as a reminder? As a rule, singing was a sign she was happy, and he knew he shouldn't comment. He didn't know when to broach the subject, or if. Some stones were best unturned, and if it was a big story, no detail spared, he didn't want to be lying there with his face to the wall in the darkness. Worse, he didn't want to be judged on the response he made or didn't.

There she was, already in bed with the duvet right up to her mouth. She barely gave him enough time to get there before she turned off the light on her side. Just when he could have felt frisky, in spite of ... or maybe because.

"You tired?" he asked.

"Yes," she said. Not yeah, or mm, or her usual grunt but a whole word, crisp. It felt decisive, but he put his arm around her anyway, finding her waist. They used to sleep naked; when did that stop? 1989 or early 90. Some facts could never be checked.

Norma had thought before of leaving. But what was out there, to replace this – his skin always just a degree or two cooler than hers, his hair always soft to touch, and the way they knitted together like continents used to? He'd know when. They hadn't drifted so many thousand miles apart, had they? It was just that they'd reshaped a bit over time so the fit had to be forced now and then and alcohol could help, memory too.

"Sometimes," she said, as she felt herself warm against him, "I still love you. Not always. And I'd rather it was lovemaking not sex if it's all the same to you."

The pause felt long. No kiss on the forehead then. No hand lowering under the duvet.

"Is that what it was, with Spandau Ballet?"

She spluttered. Was that his idea of a joke? She slapped his thigh. "Not the whole band, Brian! Not even one of them! It was the sound engineer at the Roxy I was besotted with for months, Friday to Friday. Gorgeous hair, a bit like yours was. Still is."

She touched it. His body had softened now but she wasn't perfectly sure how his face would look if she had cat's eyes through the darkness. She purred, and giggled, and took his hand in hers. His veins were turning into ridges.

"He bought me a drink and we snogged outside near the bins." She wasn't sure she wanted it, not like that. But maybe she was kidding herself, now, then. "He wasn't pretty up close. Just sweatier than a gorilla in a Batman suit and smokier than Bonfire Night. But not hot. He was high on something. It's a wonder he didn't join the wrong wires and blow the roof off the gig." She knew she might be winging it now but she was good at that; Brian couldn't do stories, not even to win the jackpot. She tried to make out the line of his mouth. "That's not a sexual metaphor. I told him thanks but no thanks."

"No one night stand?"

Was he relieved, bless him? Or cross? "Uh-uh." She waited. "I don't know why ..."

"You lied?"

He didn't ask when. She had to keep control of it now. "Oh, I don't know. Do I have to give you three reasons to choose from? Because they might all be true." He was quiet but she could feel the rhythm of him in his belly. "Think of it as sudden death, Brian. You have to find your own answer. Only you've got plenty of time."

He used to like being teased. She could smell the coconut sweetness of the Korma on his forehead where the hair fell.

"You made it up?" he checked, as if he wanted Jeremy to repeat whatever it was, the question or answer.

"Facts and stories aren't as different as you think," she told him. "Like me and you — we're not the same but we overlap."

She could wait for ever for one reason, never mind three. Or for him to tell her he loved her, but she believed it anyway, even before he kinked his leg around hers.

The track played in her head again but she beat it off with the story of the leather coat, asking Brian who played next at LiveAid. She didn't suppose he was too tired to reel off the whole running order.

He might be the one with the memory but he was a lot better at forgetting.

More about *The Simla Palace*

When my husband Leslie read this story, he came downstairs and said, "Should I be worried?!" As a portrait of a marriage that's extended beyond a Silver Wedding, it's bleak, but I was also aiming for humour – just of a rather dark kind. I hope there's a little tenderness too.

I wanted to explore memory. I'm old enough now to recognise its failings, its fuzziness, its gaps and conflations – and the power of the past in the face of all this uncertainty or even fog. Some of us retain details. Perhaps those are the quiz champions like Brian. Others, like me, hold on to the feelings. If I can rerun a scene I see and hear, that's always because it has a powerful emotional symbolism for me. In my story, Brian and Norma are two different people with different versions of their life together, and not just because much of it has been lived apart. I've adopted two voices to illustrate this, allowing them to present each other and to show how little they still understand about each other after all these years.

What happened, exactly, to Norma? You can decide. We all know about denial, about buried trauma recovered. Maybe the fact is that we can't be sure of truths, even those that are personal to us alone.

As a footnote, I captained a very unusual team on BBC2's *Eggheads* in 2016 (filmed eight months earlier), winning £29,000 for Alopecia UK. That's a story in itself. So of all the TV quiz shows, it will always be my favourite.

Series 17, Episode 20: we made Yahoo Celebrity News!

THE GOLDEN BABY

This is a tale, vividly and beautifully told, of two people who separately found the treasure, and the effect on their individual but interconnected lives, an effect that in the end is determined by their natures. You can see the snow and feel the candlelight flickering – a scene set for magic and transformation.

Trish Young, Reviewer, North Cornwall, UK

A fantasy tale that was so full of stunning description that I read it three times. Sue's characters, especially All, came to life vividly, as did the cold, deep snow setting. This story read like a fable of old and I thoroughly enjoyed it.

Michelle Briscombe, Cardiff, Wales, UK,
Author of *Silent Mountain* and *The House on March Lane*

A most enjoyable story, as strong and full as a flagon of mead, and rich and deep as the bard's velvet cloak! Travel now, to meet the Golden Baby, and see if he does appear in your dreams this night ...

Jackie Juno, Poet, comedy writer, singer and performer, Devon, UK

This reminded me of classic fairy tales I used to read as a child. Hampton is a superb author. I loved the combination of fantasy and morality story.

Melanie Strickland, Social justice campaigner, London, UK

THE GOLDEN BABY

Maybe there was a time, long ago, when nothing surprised anyone, because no one expected the earth to explain its mysteries. Besides, everyone knew that of all its truths the deepest lay in stories. So everything that happened meant one thing or perhaps another – or both, or just as probably nothing at all. Nobody imagined that a heart could hold any knowledge more universal than the smile it showed, and reasons were just notes on the wind.

So it was with the Golden Baby.

Who found it?

The child they all forgot. His name was All, because a name was all he had. It seemed he had nothing to say and nothing much to do except breathe the life around him. Inside too, for all they knew. His silence was sealed. Only feelings shook it open with sounds that might be pain or fear. Even his mother, Erin, could not read their meaning in All's eyes.

All found the Golden Baby in the snow. Or so the story went, the one he could not tell.

The snow was deep and always new. No sooner had the earth's contours been torn and grooved, scuffed and reshaped by boots and hooves, wheels and paws, than nightfall restored them. But each morning the curves swelled fuller and All's worn old boots sank deeper. The crunch they made gaped wider, like a whisper in a cave. It made him laugh inside.

The Golden Baby shone as it lay on the snow. It made no disturbance, as if the wind, like a mother, had prepared a place for it to fit. At first All thought it must be a small fire, or a crown dropped by a king. The gold was brighter than a beak or a fruit. It made him chuckle because it looked warm, but in its cradle of snow nothing melted. Nothing stirred, not even a single snowflake suspended in the bitter air.

With eager steps he sank his way towards the Golden Baby, and his heart felt hot in his chest. His cold, frayed lips spilt out a sound that wondered. The baby had fat golden arms but they didn't move. Its eyes were closed. The Golden Baby didn't shiver, any more than a bowl would tremble. No breath smoked from its perfect mouth.

All did not touch because he hated to hurt things and in any case he was afraid of how it would feel against his skin. As much as deep snow allows a clumsy boy, he ran.

The baby would not die because it didn't live.

It wouldn't cry.

It could shine without him and he would not be missed. He never was. No one needed All and All needed nothing. So he left the Golden Baby lying under the kingfisher sky, and as he fled his heart burned with every breath.

Garek went foraging, snow or no snow. There was more than one way to be a hunter and Garek had got lucky before. The dog helped, with its nose down. People were so careless with their scarves, gloves, knives … There was never any knowing what he might salvage, clean and sell. And once, a red kite had left a kill fresh enough for the fire because a female called on the wind. Garek's eyes were not as sharp as they used to be but his greed never abated, and his patience was the kind only money could nurture.

A sudden glisten or gleam always quickened his pace but what dazzled him was like a crop of light and he must harvest it.

The Golden Baby was the most precious sight of his scrabbling, scheming, scouring life. But who could have left such a treasure behind? Their loss, thought Garek, whoever they were. It was his now.

The dog hung back and barked but the baby did not cry. Garek had little education but he prided himself that he knew craftsmanship. Nonetheless, he needed to be sure. So he picked up a stick and dangled it near the Golden Baby. There was a moment when he almost expected a golden hand to close around the stick, but the baby did not move. Shaking his head at his own foolishness, Garek stroked the golden chest with his grubby glove, and shuddered. So cold! It was like touching an icicle.

Garek was wondering how much the Golden Baby might weigh, and how far he could carry it in secret, when the golden eyelids lifted and two equally golden eyes shone up at him, fiery as little suns. Stepping backwards, he gasped and the eyes closed again. Ah! Two more steps and he was leaning again above the baby. Again the eyes blazed wide, the eyeballs still as coins, or grocer's weights. It was a kind of hinge, no more, triggered by shadow. But a fine surprise! He grinned to imagine the crowds jumping as those eyes opened wide on them. They'd get their money's worth.

He could set the baby on some straw. In darkness it would stun like a relic in a church. The superstitious would say their prayers and he would take their money, a kind of fee ...

He was a caretaker, after all.

Garek picked up the baby. It was no heavier than a dead lamb. As he wrapped it in his cloak a thin trail of blood dribbled around his hand like dark red wool. A drop fell on the snow. Garek cursed, though he felt no pain and could find no sharp corners. The ragged scarlet bloom grew slowly at his feet. Garek wiped his hand on the cloak and turned his back on the snow flower he left behind.

But the air had grown colder around him and the Golden Baby slowed his steps as the sky faded to ice.

Where was the boy they called All, while the greedy old man struggled through the snow with the Golden Baby hidden in blood-specked wool?

He was lying in a fever that his mother could not cool, crying without words.

Erin never liked to come too near, in case it was true after all that there were demons inside him and they lay in wait for her, ready to seize her spirit when it was weakest.

She left him to sleep, because that was where the peace could begin. She was frightened to love him. Feeding and clothing him was her penance, her shame.

Though she hoped he might live, perhaps it was his time to die.

Garek cleared a space in his cottage. He bent a willow casket around the Golden Baby and as twilight fell he lit a candle beside it. He had to keep opening the door he'd padlocked, to wipe the baby free of any drops of blood that beaded the gold. His own fingernails were tipped with red where the blood clogged and would not wash away.

The Golden Baby lay as still as ever behind the willow bars that made its cage. Its reliquary, thought Garek, and poked the dog as it snoozed.

"Go!" he said. "Make them come."

The dog was reluctant but a few scuffs with Garek's boots sent it out of the door into the dusk. Barking, it worried at the heels of the villagers until they grew curious about Garek and what the dog's persistence meant. Perhaps the old scoundrel was sick?

Some took a slice of pie, others an apple or two. The widow who had refused his invitation to be his wife poured some fresh cider into a clay jug and hoped it would sweeten his spirit. Mumbling about the fate that might have met old Garek, they trudged through the snow to his smoky cottage with its sour old smells. Perhaps he had fallen. Perhaps they'd find him dead.

Hearing them, and with no idea how disconcertingly his narrow eyes glinted by candlelight, Garek prepared his smile. He bade them welcome and held out his hand. The money was for the church, he said, because the Golden Baby was a miracle. They would see for themselves if they handed over a nice shiny coin, maybe two. But one at a time, he insisted, because the Golden Baby must not be woken or alarmed.

Who would go first? Some hesitated. Garek encouraged the widow because she was devout, and had once seen her husband's spirit in the eye of a fish. She paid her money and Garek pushed the curtain aside. Devout as she was, Garek watched her as she approached the willow frame. He trusted no one.

At the sight of the Golden Baby the widow covered her face and moaned. Then she turned to him, and the thin old skin on her cheek seemed to reflect a little gold as her mouth opened in a quivery smile.

"Step closer," he told her.

At once her shadow was the key to open the baby's eyes. She cried out to a host of saints Garek had forgotten as she fell to her knees.

When she emerged she quivered with awe and hurried off to fetch her neighbours. The others were eager now to follow and Garek's mug soon chinked full of coins. Garek made them coffee and did not stint the beans. The Golden Baby meant he would never forage again.

One after another the pilgrims left, thanking Garek and praising gods old and new. Some were sure the crops next summer would be bounti-ful – as golden as the baby. One husband believed his wife would prove fertile after all – it was a sign! Word filtered through the village that this winter the Golden Baby would protect them from fevers and chills. The baby was an amulet, a rainbow and a posset from the apothecary, all in one! They were blessed.

Garek was most blessed of all. But he wished the blood stain would fade from his hands.

As days went by and Garek grew used to fine wine, Erin heard stories. While her strange son burned in his bed, a Golden Baby brought light to tired eyes. She had little time for magic, or for gossip either, but the darkness rimming Ali's eyes made her shudder. And once, when she was young, she had shuddered at Garek too, because his kiss was like old meat. If the glance of a Golden Baby could straighten her son and make him strong, she could rest while he worked instead. If the spell could make him handsome, he could find a wife and the pair of them could keep her warm and fed in years to come.

Tipping out the coins from a pot at the back of her cupboard, she counted them. Trusting one of them to the girl she found shaping a snowball outside her door, she told her:

"Ask Garek to bring the Golden Baby to me."

An hour later the girl returned. She shook her hair, damp with snow.

Erin plucked the pearl earrings from her ears, and dropped them in the girl's pocket. "Give him these," she said, "and I'll bake your mother some bread."

But when the girl returned, she was alone.

Erin was angry now – with the boy in his fever and the man who would have taken her honour if she'd let him. Wrapping her cloak around her, she set off for Garek's cottage.

A blizzard began, whipping her skin as one hand held the cloak tight under her chin and another clasped her money bag inside it. Most likely she'd die herself, she thought, as the numbness weighted her heart. And all this for a boy too strange for the world and much too ugly.

The evening's wine had stolen Garek's morning. Now his head pressed on him like iron and his mound of a belly groaned. In his temper, and a state of undress, he'd stoked the fire to a blaze and sent the early customers away – including the girl Erin sent to insult him. As if he'd forgotten her teasing and scorn. Such vanity, when he could have given her a son she didn't need to hide!

Then he'd slept again. Waking to the sound of snow on the wind, he scowled. Such weather would rob him and keep them all at home. Now the fire was failing. He could taste the ash in his mouth.

Rubbing his eyes, he looked across to the trap that kept the Golden Baby safe. But all he saw was splintered willow, as if a storm had blown in. Not a glimmer of gold. The baby had gone and in its place were splashes of blood, dark on straw.

Wide-awake, Garek thrashed around his cottage, as if the baby might be in a cupboard with his pans. With the bolt in place on his door, no earthly force could have broken in. Seized by fear, he shook the chest where his fortune rattled, reassured by its music and its weight. But his anger did not abate.

So when Erin knocked, he refused to answer. When she banged on his shutters and called his name, he sat rigid in his chair.

"I bring more than money," she called.

Garek remembered the pretty way she used to tilt her head on her long neck, and smile as if she knew more than all the men of the world could ever suspect. He remembered the fullness of her breasts and hips.

He lifted the latch and opened the door.

Stirring in his bed, All smiled, though he did not know why. He could smell the snow in the air outside, and sense it, thick as armour, on the roof. Stretching, he felt a song inside him, light as lace. When he climbed out of bed he did not shiver. The cottage was warm, and brightly lit as if the sun shone in. He opened the shutters, one hand shading his eyes.

The boy called All saw the Golden Baby curled up like a cat on his doorstep. The sound streaming through the sunlight was an appeal, and to All it spoke of loneliness. Had no one taken care of the baby? Wouldn't it be cold and hungry? This time he wouldn't leave it to the whole, upright people. Even a broken boy could give it love.

Looking down on it, he grinned as its eyes opened wide and its arms lifted. Carefully, because he knew how clumsy his limbs tried to be, he reached his own awkward arms around the Golden Baby. He stumbled, his balance lost, and fell stupidly to the floor, while the golden light flooded over him in a pool. Like gold in a furnace his body felt molten now. With a rush of strength he rose to his feet. Now there was no baby, just a burst of flowers rising crimson from the snow.

"Where are you?" he cried as the light dimmed and the snow began to thread through the wind. The song inside him traced its way out like a bird from a nest.

The Golden Baby had gone, but when the boy they called All glimpsed himself in his mother's mirror, he smiled. His legs still bent, his arms didn't match and his chest was narrow. But his eyes shone. He picked a few of the flowers and put them in a little vase to surprise his mother when she came home. The rest he left to blaze.

Did the snow bury the Golden Baby? Garek thought so. Fierce with determination, he set out to uncover it, burn it and melt it into money. No more extracting paltry pennies from the poor! The baby would make him a duke, a count, a king! For months he dug his way through drifts and blizzards, until his body ached and his spirit chilled hard inside him.

When the snow claimed another secret for the future to scavenge, no one missed him – least of all Erin, who had banned him from her bed.

What of the villagers and their hopes? Many bore fruit, and some of them rotted as fruit will do, but some, cherry-sweet, bent branches low in Spring. There were births and weddings to bind them, and All sang at every one of them. With time Erin faded, losing everything but the music he made and the warmth of his touch.

"My golden boy," she said, in the armchair he'd built her, and patted his hand.

If there was a meaning in the mystery, no one named it. Memories melted into folk tales with added rubies, a troll and a wizard in a cave. But ribboning through the decades shone a tune, laden with wordless verses. And only All could sing it, because truth was all he knew.

More about *The Golden Baby*

This is the odd one out in many ways. When reading Kazuo Ishiguro's *The Buried Giant* I decided it would be fun to attempt the same kind of style. I admit I abandoned the novel, but for other reasons to do with losing the plot, which I put down to my failure rather than Ishiguro's. So my story has the feel of one told around a fire, and it's set long ago and nowhere in particular, because this is the familiar world of the fable, with magic and mystery.

Ever since writing my alopecia novel *The Waterhouse Girl* I've been drawn to characters with any kind of difference that challenges them and makes them vulnerable to rejection. Of course the genre, while distinctive, carries with it a freedom to luxuriate in imagery and symbols that real-world contemporary stories couldn't accommodate. Writing this one was a powerfully multi-sensory experience and I hope that comes across to the reader. As for its meanings, I knew more about those once I'd found my ending. I'd like to think that we'll always be drawn to such lyrical fantasies, with their long tradition, even as adults hardened by a very different world.

VISITING MISS LYON

A young woman struggling to find her place in the world encounters an old woman fighting her secret guilt. A story of quiet gestures and things left unsaid, Visiting Miss Lyon *is both sombre and playful, poignant and hopeful.*

Sarah Butler, Manchester, UK,
Author of *Ten Things I've Learnt About Love* and *Before the Fire*

Sue paints vivid images in the mind with this short story. It uses an original concept developed with haste but not unduly so. I enjoy this author for her creative skill in using words as if they were paints on a varied palette – this story is a good example.

John Carver, British Electronic Test Engineer and author, Bucks, UK

Visiting Miss Lyon *is a gentle, 'feel good' tale interwoven with humour. The protagonist, Anna, is the daughter every mother would aspire to – warm, considerate and touchingly empathetic. Bittersweet, heart-lifting and poignant!*

Melanie Whipman, Surrey, UK, Associate Lecturer at the University of Chichester and author of the short story collection, *Llama Sutra*

The narrator, who is a bit of a fish out of water in her first year at university in an era of Afghan coats and casual sex, finds new purpose when she starts making regular visits to a local old people's home. The story charts her growing confidence, culminating in an audacious attempt to bring peace of mind to the home's most troubled, and troubling, resident. Sue Hampton conveys the narrator's awkwardness beautifully, and engages the reader's sympathies for all of the players in this drama, from the elderly people who draw her into their world to the irritable neighbour with a short attention span.

Nicky Coates, Singer-songwriter, Bristol, UK

VISITING MISS LYON

When I signed up with Jill during Freshers' Week, I'd just been singing *The Family of Man*. At that point I'd no idea the family included Miss Lyon. I was a child at eighteen, so as we arrived at Rutherford Lodge, I was glad to be back-up for Jill. Chaplain had said that in any old people's home, visitors mattered most on Sunday afternoons. Or rather, their absence did.

The place was shabby, but with fewer spores than the bathroom on my corridor and no smells grimmer than boiled cabbage. Acutely aware of the distance that separated me from my own family, I tried to imagine being adrift – not from choice, setting off on a train with a trunk and a grant and a promise to write every week, but because no one cared. We were there for the abandoned.

Jill found some bright sparks called Lily and Ted. I was sent over to Edith, whose silent rocking was off-putting. But I talked very softly, touching her lightly on the arm – until she stopped. Which was thrilling, but not for long, because in walked Miss Lyon with her zimmer frame and a dark, leathery stare. Even before she was lowered into her arm-chair, she'd begun to yell. And Jill's grin soon changed to a *get me out of here* expression as visiting families tried to ignore the scattergun assault.

Miss Lyon was disturbed, and disturbing: "I'm going to Hell, I am!" or "It's the fire and brimstone for me!" All accompanied by tears – not loud, but slow and steady down a George Eliot nose. Venturing near enough to say hello, I thought about placing my hand on hers but didn't take the risk in case it jerked up and struck me. And I felt sure it would be cold as death already.

Five minutes later I followed Jill down the path to the street. A man with a lawnmower and an arm full of cuttings greeted us with a wink and a Benny Hill grin. Looking at Jill, I knew those weren't for me. But if she was smiling at the attention, that smile soon faded.

"Someone should have warned us," she said.

"What do you think she did?" I asked, but I didn't really want to guess. We talked about Ted's sense of humour and Lily's baby skin, how sad it was that they had no family to call on them once in a while. But that was the point; it meant volunteers were needed, valued.

So I wasn't best pleased when Jill cried off the next Sunday, just because she'd got off with a bloke at the college bop, a Third Year P.E. type, and ... well, I didn't need to know the rest. On arrival I heard my name called out by Ted, so I chatted with him about Fulham – or rather, let him report on the season so far. When Edith was wheeled in I sat with her, trying to head off the rocking but not sure my words were understood. It was the sound that mattered, the tone, and the touch.

"She likes you," said a member of staff offering me tea in the same green cup and saucer they had at my church back home. I eased away, still murmuring, unable to face Miss Lyon and avoiding eye contact as she sat at the back as stiff as Lot's wife.

Lily was smiling at the children around the neighbouring chair; she saw me and reached for an embrace. I explained why Jill wasn't with me, disinclined to make excuses for her. Lily's pale blue eyes widened with delight.

"Have you got a beau?" Lily asked. I may have blushed. "A young man. Are you courting?"

"I've never had a boyfriend," I admitted. Lily was all pity and encouragement. She'd had plenty herself, she said, before she met Mr Right. She showed me photographs of grandchildren in Australia, dressed for the beach. When she asked whether there was any nice student I had my eye on, I began to tell her the truth. I had a growing crush on a Drama student called Luke, who'd been cast for the lead in the Christmas production of *Jesus Christ Superstar* – even though with his long blond hair and small beard he looked more Californian than Arabic. And exactly like the pictures in my first ever Bible.

"Get yourself a part, dear!" Lily told me. "I would."

But I couldn't have said a line on stage without rattling, and if I shared a scene with Luke I didn't suppose I'd be able to breathe.

That was when Miss Lyon stopped staring at the flocked wallpaper.

"I'm a sinner!" she called, her voice taut with agitation and her clawed fists beating her thighs. "Beyond the pale!"

One of the smaller children clung to his mother. Was she calling me, I

82

wondered? Did she need an audience, or a priest?

"Ignore her, dear," said Lily. "We have to."

But I had to try. For ten minutes, maybe fifteen, I listened to the same record, as if the needle was stuck on her wickedness and the punishment to come. "I'm sure you won't, Miss Lyon," I told her when she said where she was doomed to spend eternity. "We all do things we're sorry for," I reassured her, for all the difference it made. And when I said I must go now, she yelled after me with a power surge that shocked me and probably terrified the children: "You don't know what I've done!"

Before the next visit I prayed for help. I could have put an essay first, or let my first ever hangover stop me, but it was a commitment and I'd have been ashamed to let Chaplain down. Over the weeks, the predictability of the pattern made me feel less jagged.

As Christmas approached I tried to persuade Jill to join me after lectures one weekday. "Lily wants to know all about your love life."

She pulled a face. "I don't think she does."

"She had sex too, you know," I muttered, wondering whether personally I ever would. I hadn't even enjoyed my first attempts at snogging. Stroking Edith was safer, and felt more loving too.

"It's too depressing," Jill said. "Especially the old sinner. You'd think they'd give her tranquillisers."

I couldn't really argue with that. I'd begun to wish Jill wasn't in the room next to mine even before she added, "On the subject of my love life, I got off with Luke last weekend." Her smile blazed, triumphant. I walked away blinded.

The home had been festively decorated for a few weeks but that evening carols were playing, every note soprano. I could smell mince pies and mulled wine as I entered the lounge, and the huge tree in the corner was strung with tinsel and heavily baubled. I assumed all the armchairs had been shifted to make room until I realised Edith's was missing. I turned to Ted, who waved cheerfully.

"Anna! Merry Christmas, love. Join the party."

I waved to Lily, who was singing along to *In The Bleak Midwinter*, her eyes shining.

"Edith?" I asked.

"Dead," Ted told me, his voice flat. "Couldn't stop crying after they took Miss Lyon away. Then when she stopped, everything else stopped too."

I looked. Two chairs missing. "Miss Lyon? You mean she's in hospital?"

"The loony bin, love. Not before time, poor old girl."

He reached stiffly for a plate of mince pies and held it towards me, his hand shaking.

"No, thank you." The room was hot and the spiced wine made me want to give up a habit I'd only just begun.

Glad as I was to hear that Ted's son was flying back from JFK that night, I stood as soon as he paused. I wished everyone a barely audible happy Christmas and found a member of staff emerging from the office with festive food filling one cheek.

He told me where they'd taken Miss Lyon and I realised I passed it on the bus every time I went into town. But he warned me off too, adding that she was in "quite a state".

"Can you tell me," I asked, "what ... I mean why ...?"

"Her dark sin? If anyone knew that, it was poor Edith, and I don't think it helped either of them."

Maybe if *One Flew Over the Cuckoo's Nest* had been released a year later I might have gone out for a cider or two instead, but I was on a mission now. I ran as much of the distance back to campus as I could and found Jill's door locked. But I could hear her. And him.

I banged on the door and when she opened it, I told her I needed Luke. Holding the door, she made sure I didn't get a glimpse of his body. As I called in to him, trying to explain, she kept butting in and telling me I was crazy too. Then she called me a jealous bitch and slammed the door pretty much in my face.

On the corridor I just stood helplessly because Edith was dead and it was supposed to be Christmas and Luke was naked with my best friend. I was face down on my own bed when I heard a knock, and there he was, barefoot in his flared jeans, pulling his jumper over static-frizzed hair.

"All right," he said. "I'll do it. It'd be a rehearsal."

He wore his Afghan coat on top of the costume and I gave him a mint

84

so Miss Lyon wouldn't smell the smoke on his breath. We didn't bother to wait for a bus, and he didn't get a chance to say much as we walked because I splurged, and cried too.

When we arrived, it wasn't like the home. No crimson anywhere, or cinnamon in the air. They didn't want to let us see her because we weren't family but my tears made the Red Sea part. We followed directions. Outside the room, I stood and waited for a while because she wasn't shouting and that unnerved me. She was drugged but I couldn't feel any peace, any respite. She didn't see us hiding around the door. And then as we watched she stiffened, as if the nightmare had just resumed. In her eyes the terror burned back.

"I'm sorry, I'm sorry!" she murmured. "I don't want to go!" She turned her face into her pillow. I took Luke's warm coat, sent him on stage in his long white tunic and hoped his acting was as good as Jill said.

On my seat out of sight I heard him; he was pretty convincing. He didn't sing *Everything's All Right* the way he reassured the disciples in the cave but that was more or less what he told her. He remembered the script: repentance, forgiven, Heaven. I had an idea that he might have placed his hand on hers but I had to imagine that, just as I'd often imagined how it would feel against my cheek, on my breast. And we both cried: Miss Lyon in her bed with Jesus holding her hand and me hugging his coat. A surprised nurse came to intervene but the scene had worked its power. Luke beckoned. I looked in and saw Miss Lyon had closed her eyes and her mouth had made a new shape.

"Thank you," I whispered.

Luke held me a minute before he told me I needed locking up too, and smiled. On our quiet walk back to college our hands swung very close between us.

"You're coming to the show?" he checked as we parted, and I lied. I heard next day – not from Jill, she was avoiding me – that he was fabulous.

Checking my pigeon hole with my trunk behind me, I found a note from Chaplain asking me to drop by before I left. Sitting me down, he said Miss Lyon had died peacefully minutes after our visit. I told him everything and he just nodded and blessed me. Soon I was on the train, wondering as I looked at my reflection who I really was and who I might become.

My faith was red velvet curtains I could close and feel snug. Now it's more of a ladder in old tights. If I end up in a home I hope there'll be visitors on a Sunday but I never had children, just taught a few thousand over the years. I found Luke on Facebook and he didn't marry Jill, not even the third time. There's a chance Google might know what Miss Lyon had to forgive but we don't need facts to understand.

More about *Visiting Miss Lyon*

The seed of this story came from my own student experience of visiting such a home back in the Seventies, and talking to an old lady who cried about going to hell and refused to accept my assurances that she wouldn't. She was hard to like and didn't seem to have any friendships there. As an innocent and rather devout girl with a protected upbringing I was out of my depth and pretty distressed but also desperate to help. I was a huge fan of a certain rock opera that had become a movie when I was at school. In fact, my best friend and I had sat through a short film on Delft pottery one day, in order to watch *Jesus Christ Superstar* twice. I can still sing along with all the words. At the time I'm not sure I registered that Jesus shouldn't have been a Californian blond, probably because on the charity collection box that sat by the phone through my childhood, that's exactly how he looked. It was how I grew up imagining him.

The friend who accompanied me to the home was, and still is, an angel, so the rest of the story is fiction and Anna isn't me. But my student days still remain, like Anna's, thick with vivid and emotive memories. I'm sure that in different ways, they shaped me.

SUE HAMPTON

A LITERARY FIGURE

As ever, I find myself stunned by the elegance of Sue's prose, which manages at once to be as light as air and ocean deep, while also paying homage to its allegorical inspiration. This is a moving meditation on writing, loving, and growing old; a life beautifully observed, this is short story writing at its finest.

Stephen Carver, Norwich, UK, Head of Online Courses at the Unthank School of Writing, reader/mentor for The Literary Consultancy, freelance editor, & cultural historian. Author of *Shark Alley: The Memoirs of a Penny-a-Liner*

A Literary Figure is intriguing with a good balance between food-for-thought and a reader's satisfaction with the ending. I've heard, short stories written by skilled authors condense meaning into a small space; similar to a Haiku, where the author strips away all but the necessary. I decided I would read the story twice. First I read it through very fast, but a few paragraphs in, I knew the story was interesting and well written. So then I read through slowly, absorbing and enjoying all the nuances, and the jumps through time. The story is intriguing. My concern that I may be left hanging at the end of 3000 words did not come to fruition. The story felt complete, leaving me with just the right balance between food-for-thought and a reader's satisfaction with the end of the story.

From A Bookish Observation: by Diane Challenor, Book Blogger, Artuccino.com Australia

A LITERARY FIGURE

Accustomed as she was to shining academically, Georgia found submission a desolate business. Her art, craft, sweat and all-consuming commitment had, it seemed, merely generated a product – for a market in which talent and intellect were poor substitutes for celebrity. Shaken to find that even her realistic expectations had left her unprepared for bone fide reality, Georgia reflected that the world was not, in any way she could think of, remotely as she would wish it; why should publishing be any different?

The agent's unconvincing gush made way for evasion and vagueness. So in the end, the email acceptance exceeded expectation with a wildness that felt heady. It was the process itself that at one point she thought she might not survive. The sight of her work viciously tracked in red might have made a Victorian swoon with or without a bodice, but remembering the anti-depressants in her bathroom cabinet Georgia had to remind herself that she'd struggled too hard for independence from their magic to surrender again at the first assault. That was the word that struck her as she opened the attachment on her laptop to see her words slashed through and mutilated. "But maybe too literary?" Suzie the agent had suggested from the start, with the brightest of lifts at the end of the query. Every one of eighty-seven thousand words had arisen from the ashes of countless others over three and a half years. "It's been intensively edited," she'd said, with the kind of cool understatement she tried, when the commitment felt too emotional to control, to bring to her work.

"Don't compromise one word," Ted told her, playing to a non-existent gallery. He hadn't read any one of those words in question. "No one messes with my sister."

But at the end of negotiations she didn't know what kind of account to give. Had she won more than she'd lost? Was she deluding herself about the benefits of concessions made or the necessity of resistance?

"It is what it is," she'd told Ted, unable to explain.

"You're a writer, Georgia," he said, pushing back that floppy hair more angrily than usual. "What the hell does that mean? Are you talking about the novel you love more than life? Or should that verb be in the past tense, now that some pipsqueak editor has reshaped it for you in the light of his own ignorance?"

Georgia wished she could pat his hand, still almost a fist, but he was a virtual brother at the time, thanks to Skype. So she just said, "I love you, Ted."

It was a declaration that, with a caveat about his perturbingly Tory politics, prompted a kind of snort through the family nose. Georgia's was even longer and a little overwhelming – especially on train journeys that reminded her, as she tried to gaze past it, of an identity she preferred not to own.

But they needed a photo for the book, they said.

"Is that necessary?" she asked. "Can I not be mysterious, and androgynous? G.E. Lott. I think I sound like a bank manager from the days when you picked up the phone and someone was on the party line."

As if anyone at the publishers remembered such a thing. She was too old for a debut and too ugly for a digital age.

"The trolls are out!" Ted told her, once the publicity hit social media with the best image from a long and distressing shoot. "*The horse no one wants to ride!* Bastards!"

She wouldn't have known, since nothing could have persuaded her onto Twitter. He'd already pointed out that she'd exceed the character limit in her first three words.

"Inevitably," she said.

"Morons," he declared, and went into battle in brief skirmishes.

The shortlists were validation of a kind and the prize hurled her sleeplessly into a brief period of elation, until it became clear that she was expected to attend a ceremony described as glitzy, in clothes from the same register. Georgia sent Ted. He was both infinitely more charming and a great deal fonder of overhyped champagne. He even promised to read the book very soon.

As for sales, they were modest, which did at least spare her the kind of fame that would have held her captive indoors for fear of paparazzi.

"The book's not an easy read," her editor said, having decimated the novel's syllable count and halved the length of most of its sentences. As if Georgia's dedication to exploring the human interior in all its enthralling complexity made her guilty of something far more problematic than the coke habit Ted ascribed to all worlds he called artsy.

She met Henry at a dinner party after thinking better of claiming a headache. "Rabid radical," said Ted. "Fulminates against neoliberalism in a professorial way that's hard to counter."

"I noticed," said Georgia, who hadn't tried. Henry's eloquence had been irresistible. But she'd talked, invited and in unusual detail, about her work; he'd promised, as people did, to read the book, but with eyes so alive she hoped he meant it.

"Not what you'd call an Adonis," Ted said, with a grin she thought cruel.

"I'm much more interested in ideas," she retorted, "than biceps, six-packs or Beckham beauty."

No, she reported, his wife had been poorly that night. Georgia didn't confess to the late-night online search that had found this missing spouse taller and prettier than Henry, if considerably less than his intellectual equal. Soon, at the end of an email about climate injustice and the role of the arts in awakening resistance, Henry emailed that in all terms but legal, his marriage had died.

Six weeks later he moved in. She thought Ted's outrage would dissipate but it had a new force and a crueller coldness – so steely that he couldn't express it except through unanswered texts and unreturned calls.

"It's because I've taken you," Henry said. "It's that passionate intensity you Lotts go in for. I bet Teddy behaved the same way over Lego wheels."

She told herself her brother couldn't spoil this; nothing could, not even the News. Surprised by winter sun in bed one morning, Georgia lay still and watched Henry until he woke.

"So this is love," she said.

"It must be," he agreed. "And yes, I'm glad in this instance – isolated as it is – to be proved wrong."

About the romantic illusion, he meant: the fairy tale. Georgia stroked the black hair from his forehead, admiring its smoothness while hers swelled unmanageably around her, not so much silky in its abundance as raw against skin.

As they kissed she wondered for a moment whether he might find the stamina for the kind of lovemaking she would not dare to write. But this was their fifth decade and he was under more medication than he liked to admit – or take, without her to insist.

"Am I a hussy," she asked him, "because I'd love to just lie here with you until nightfall?"

"Teatime? And then what, hussy?"

"You know what."

Sometimes she thought her brain had been consumed in the fire, and left molten without shape. But then she would sit in her dressing gown at the kitchen table, and wear away at the keyboard until her third mug of tea had cooled and hunger became so overwhelming that it shaded into anger. She had to open some baked beans to soak her toast before she read back the pages on screen, or the whole would be at risk from highlight and delete.

"Get some fresh air," he'd tell her as he left for the university. "Clothes, exercise, conversation over coffee. Breaks, Georgia. Promise." And sometimes, "Look after yourself when I'm gone."

By the time his heart failed, she had four novels, three awards and a fairly substantial Wikipedia profile. A critic had just described her as 'publicity-shy, political and unfathomably religious, and by some accounts, difficult' after she'd declined to be interviewed.

Light broke out like bird flu amongst the literati who now recognised Henry's talent as a disciplined philosopher in an age of soundbites. They might have said a thinker, thought Georgia; that would be more than enough to set him apart from the profiteers. But she succeeded in keeping his death a private matter until she'd watched him lowered into the natural burial site in his biodegradable coffin. With only his rigidly silent son and grim-jawed sister for company, Georgia might have hurled herself down to fit alongside him – if not for a multi-faith celebrant named Mary Angell, whose eyes smiled as if the Earth was lucky to be fed by a soul of such size.

Ted didn't know. When he read the obituary he sent white lilies, forgetting that the scent spirited her up like the Rapture and left her body struggling to stand.

She found, searching for a twenty-first century definition of religion, an unexpected question: *Is Google the new religion?* Not hers, at any rate. Georgia clung to faith in the beauty of the human soul, but was it a constant like a blood group or as unstable as weight, and could it endure the kind of old age that decayed the brain? She despaired of language, its impotence, fog and clumsiness, when as an artist or sculptor, a composer or dancer she might have breathed colour and form into an essence of truth that rose and swelled beyond words.

"I'm sad, Henry," she told the empty house. "But we haven't been parted. I hold you. You hold me."

When Ted turned up without warning, because he was "in the area" he stood and let her feel his heat and substance. She made him tea and held his hand, surprised that she hadn't forgotten any detail of their contours.

It was three years later, soon after the launch of 'her least rewarding but most ambitious novel' about young, rich, white Danny embracing the Muslim roots from his distant past, that she met Jon. Unsure at first whether he was genuinely a fan or the kind of writer who sought credibility by association, Georgia was disturbed by the person she became in his presence: shallow, almost flirtatious, more eager to amuse than challenge. He was little more than a boy to a mature woman of near-pensionable age but Georgia had never been interested in toys, especially pretty ones. She suspected him almost as deeply as she suspected herself.

One afternoon he suggested a walk in the woods, and had to be asked to slow his puppy-like pace. At the foot of a tree he warned her was far too wide to think of hugging, he knelt careless of mud and asked her to marry him.

"That's ridiculous," she said, adding as he stood that his knee had darkened with leaf mould.

Peeling it off, he cried, "What the …?"

"Gently! It's a caterpillar."

He smiled as she cupped it in her hands and watched it curl and stretch in miniature.

"I suppose you think that has a soul too."

"Bigger than yours," she told him.

Moments later he kissed her and shrugged her cardigan from her shoulder, one hand receiving a breast that had never seemed older. She pulled away.

"Caterpillars might be even less welcome on other organs," she suggested. "Apart from which, I'm sixty. I have cellulite, flaps and creases and seborrheic keratosis."

"I'm excited by your mind," he said, moving in and pressing, stroking.

This time she pushed, surprised by her strength. "It's not my mind you'll see on the pillow each morning when you wake."

"That's a yes, then!" he cried, and danced around the tree like a Hollywood Sioux.

Ted approved; they shared something she couldn't quite name and didn't understand. Jon shunned politics of every kind, preferring culture high and low. His appetite was in many ways endless – but not for the veganism she'd only recently embraced with an environmentalist's conviction.

When he mentioned a Venice honeymoon she said, "Only by train. You know I've forsworn flying." She was implacable, but compromised on the wedding with a registry office quickie.

The journey was long and expensive but she luxuriated in the views, made notes and took photographs on her old camera. He slept, seemed drawn to his tablet and called his publisher about the short story collection. Georgia had been wondering how to begin the conversation about restructuring, slackness, distance and predictability.

The hotel manager all but bowed, used the word 'illustrious' and 'prevailed upon' her for a photo to show his mother who 'adored' her work. Their second floor suite, which was showered with flowers, overlooked the Grand Canal. Jon didn't appreciate talk of the city being drowned as the planet's temperatures rose and climate change could no longer be arrested. That night in a king-sized bed they faced different walls with an expanse of cold, crisp sheet between them. Georgia lay stunned. *I am the caterpillar*, she told herself, *to be knocked from the leaf mould. And I will not cling.*

In the morning she woke to sounds she could not have identified to find her new husband jumping into the green water below. Screaming as the net curtains stirred after him, Georgia could only run to the balcony, find the phone and call room service for help.

"Mio marito e morto," she said, the words vibrato but hushed.

He was depressed, he said, in the Italian hospital bed.

"I have a history I should have told you about: medication, psychotherapy. No previous jumps into waterways."

Yes, she thought, because she had told him everything: Henry's enduring hold, her father's disapproval of flesh and candour, her mother's scattergun accusations in urine-soured dementia and Ted's on-off love. She'd even exposed the bruises from strategic engagements with the agent, editors and words.

Georgia gave him both hands. "Now you have love," she said, feeling emptiness drag the speech to the recently-mopped floor. She would live the lie for his sake, because he admired her interior, not her shell. Her 'university set text' reputation no longer aroused him but perhaps he would continue to believe in her greatness. It might be enough.

The arthritis was nothing; her fingers could still tap the keyboard and regular Reiki eased body and mind. But diseased kidneys meant oedema, swollen ankles couldn't really be hidden under long skirts Jon called hippy, and weight loss was no compensation. Tightness of breath put an end to her rare public appearances. Besides, the headaches were often overbearing. Dialysis, the doctor said. Not yet, she told him.

There were days when she lay in bed with her notebook and pen, hearing Jon write with the benefit of backspace and cut and paste. But he was coy about his subject until one day he admitted, "About you! What else? The definite biography of the brilliant but elusive Georgia Lott."

"I hope you're not counting on fame or fortune," she retorted.

She saw he was aggrieved – that she expressed no delight or gratitude. But perhaps he didn't detect her hurt, stemming from doubts he hadn't understood. She tried to smile, too faintly and too late. She determined to find the stamina for an editor's role, if he would allow her to fill it.

"I'll be forgotten," she said. Ted had reported that on a TV quiz show she was already a *Pointless* answer.

"Don't be ridiculous. I married a genius; it's my claim to fame."

She was relentlessly curious.

"You can read it when I've finished," he told her a fortnight before surgery.

The following afternoon was a Sunday. Ted and his third wife called with "an extortionately priced raw vegan cake from Covent Garden as a send-off."

Georgia had intended to get up and dressed to pour the tea but instead Ted had to sit on the bed. He held a glass of champagne in his hand and had to be told for a second time that she couldn't join him.

"To you, George," he said. "Get well soon. It's time you wrote a blockbuster."

Georgia didn't mention the biography, fearing that it would almost certainly trigger another brotherly walk-out on her life.

"Ted," she began.

"It's all right. I forgave you long ago."

"For Henry?" she began. "Are you judge and jury, Ted, the archangel at God's right hand?"

He shook his head. "Not Henry! No rules in affairs of the heart and all that. I should know."

So he meant *Unequal*. Still he smarted over her debut novel about the girl who loved her brother so much more intensely and loyally than he loved her. Because he didn't know how to receive such love; it was excess to his requirements.

"Ted, my soul nourishes my work but it's an under-the-soil kind of business. I don't flash my life across the pages."

"I don't believe you. But I forgive you anyway."

She died in her sleep that night, and no obituary was ready to roll. Jon's Twitter tribute, beginning *Goodbye my sweet inspiration* briefly held the bottom of the trending list, until the drummer of a Seventies band died in suspicious circumstances.

More about *A Literary Figure*

I've loved George Eliot, who was born Marian Evans, since I was sixteen. Of all my heroines (who include Meryl Streep, Nina Simone and Sylvie Guillem, and any number of women writers from the last hundred years along with Caroline Lucas), she means the most to me. It began with her work: novels read several times through my life, every one of them admired and savoured intellectually and every one of them a rich emotional experience. I felt that mysterious connection, as I met her characters and engaged with her stories, with the voice behind it all: her literary and human presence. Then, when I found out more about her and her life, the connection gained a rationale. As a podgy, frizzy-haired and uncool schoolgirl, I identified with the woman who felt ugly – even before I lost my hair. I was studious and academic too, and fervent in my Christianity. And of course I wanted to be a novelist, the kind that, like her, explored the human psyche and spirit as well as the bigger social picture.

In my short story I wanted to find a parallel within the constraints of contemporary living and thinking, and to expose the shallowness of a book world obsessed with sales, Hollywood and awards. I found that it's harder to work with a plotline than a blank screen. Of course I also wanted to find a style that borrowed a little of the elegant formality of the late nineteenth century, but knew that modern taste has little appetite for its expansiveness. It's a tribute, and inevitably it can't do Eliot's genius anything like justice, but I felt I owed her the attempt.

ON TRACK

What a lovely idea. A series of vignettes apparently all about one person but describing four people through their projections. Their lives and their dreams come alive in their heads, as they do for each of us. A great example of how our thoughts create our reality. I adore the line "But it was no good blaming the tree for being an acorn once, and a dragonfly didn't need to apologise for its days as a wingless nymph."

Tania Clarke, Herts, UK, Psychotherapist and coach

All of life is here, vivifying, varied and richly condensed: the ageing hippy; the disaffected youth; the exhausted City worker; the unappreciated house-wife. The lives and imaginations of these varied characters brush against each other, revealing the selves hidden beneath the labels, and, together, this community becomes so much more than the sum of its parts. I thoroughly enjoyed it.

Emma-Claire Sweeney, Herts, UK,
Author of *Owl Song at Dawn*, named as Amazon Rising Star and Hive Rising Writer 2016, shortlisted for Book Hugger Book of the Year

I loved this "slice of life" story. A wonderful piece of writing. Clever, funny, witty, engaging and gentle, but with a pertinent and perceptive observation.

Rosemary Hill, Bucks, UK, Theatre and film director

I love it! On Track certainly makes the point that no one's life is as it seems to be and our own experiences will inevitably colour our perception of other people. Sue Hampton has caught the mood of each character so well. Being a part time songwriter, I'm always trying to find neater, clearer ways of telling a story or putting across an idea. I need to keep reading her work for lessons, and it's no hardship.

Liz Lawley, Herts, UK, Ex-librarian

ON TRACK

Frances couldn't keep up with him, which was disconcerting. And watching his woven, Peruvian-style rucksack, which bumped softly against his back, made her shopping feel heavier. With his thick white beard he reminded her of Captain Birdseye, but there was nothing rosy or rounded about him. Ahead of her – and further ahead with every stride – his loose, wildly patterned shirt swelled as wind sneaked inside. Frances imagined hip bones underneath it, jutting like rock-climbing holds above his narrow waist. But no one would think him frail. In his tight drainpipe trousers he had an elastic step, flashing scarlet socks between his hems and denim sneakers. How old could he be?

As he glanced in her direction, checking for traffic, she saw a nose that novelists used to call aquiline. His face was tight, tanned and angular – and his gaze focused. No daydreaming, no autopilot. He had what the *Strictly* judges called intent.

A roadie, she guessed, for a punk band breaking at the end of the Seventies. Fit enough to lug the equipment but sharp enough to drive the van. It reminded Frances of her gigging days, before Cynthia got pregnant and Julia starting drinking for three. But as *The Mirabelles*, theirs were gentle tunes. Music fronted by this guy, now crossing the road as if cops were tailing him, would be fast, staccato, rebellious.

Maybe he was the drummer! Frances had loved a drummer once, but he wasn't impressed by melodies – or lyrics either. And rhythm soon lost its charge without them. She pictured herself in his bed, tears on silent, skin left to dry and burn a little. Was this guy hard too? She supposed she only associated softness with plenty of flesh because of the weight she'd gathered around her own bones since she was on the road with the girls. It was so long ago, it must be time for a reunion. She must get in touch.

Where was Whitebeard going in such a hurry – to an old wife watching daytime TV? Would he be minding grandchildren after school or was he more of a Ronnie Wood sort of oldie, with a young girlfriend waiting in bed? Whatever he was up to, it was brisk and it made her lethargic, as if her life force leaked away as his charged.

Now he turned a corner by the Town Hall and was gone. She'd never know. But he'd taken her somewhere she hadn't been for a while and it made her ... not sad exactly, but wistful. The grandchildren would be amazed, even shocked, if they knew what she'd got up to as a Mirabelle. But it was no good blaming the tree for being an acorn once, and a dragonfly didn't need to apologise for its days as a wingless nymph.

Had Skinny Jim Redsocks looked happy? Not really. Who did? Gardeners, florists, hairdressers mostly. Not musicians who'd been found only to be lost again, or binned. Frances wasn't sure her drummer would have worked out any worse than Tony, who'd mislaid her too over the years, forgotten through all those shared suppers and nights. And now that neither of them had a job to go to, she'd catch him looking at her as if he didn't really know where she'd come from, or been.

Redsocks knew what he thought and wanted. You could see that in his step. Frances couldn't be sure where she'd put her shopping list but chilli or shepherd's pie, carrots or peas, it didn't make much difference. Maybe she'd serve up egg and oven chips and wait for the reaction. Before that, there was an album she hadn't played for as long as she could remember, and she was going to sing along with every word.

*

It was a quiet shift so far. Behind the counter at the Oxfam shop, Lobo was thinking about Shani when the door swung open and shut – with so much force it banged the wall and rattled the nearest box in the window display: the board game from way back before his dad was a boy. The customer didn't seem to notice the noise, or Lobo when he said, "Morning," the way the manager trained volunteers to do. He just marched straight in, past the Fair Trade products towards the second-hand jewellery locked up in the glass display towers. Looking for what? Or was he about to pull a brick from inside his shirt, and smash and grab enough brooches and earrings to kit out a Nursing Home?

Lobo wouldn't mind the old guy's patchwork waistcoat but not over the crazy shirt. That looked like a jigsaw put together all wrong. Nobody would book him as a Santa in spite of the white beard; he'd scare the kids. Scrawny. Kind of fierce-looking too. Retired now, maybe, but from what? Drug-dealing?

"Can I help?" asked Lobo, pushing back his hair where it always hung

100

with just a few degrees' tilting.

The guy didn't turn. He was squinting at the jewellery as if he was trying to recognise stolen goods. Except he looked more like the burglar than the cop.

"Looking for anything particular, sir?"

Lobo had got an A in Drama and the day went faster if he played someone else. Not Loony Lobo, the geek the girls saw right through.

"You're all right," said the guy, without looking his way.

That was good to know and Lobo wished more people realised all right was what he was. Or could be, if they understood.

"Do you ever get anything really fancy?" asked Old Dope Pusher. "You know, Duchessy?"

Like a tiara? "Not really," said Lobo. "At least, I'm only here once a week. Do you want me to call the manager?"

"No, you're all right, kid. No worries, thanks."

And he'd gone, with another swing-clunk-wobble, leaving behind a smell that wasn't dope or smoke. More like grass, the green kind. And peppermint. That was a plant – Lobo had seen it on *Countryfile*, his mum's favourite.

Maybe Old Dope Pusher mowed the lawns at a hotel or a Home. There had been a big red ride-on swerver where Lobo had been. He used to watch it from his room and wish he was a boy because then it would be exciting like it used to be when his dad took him to the Railway Museum and they allowed him in the front where they used to shovel in the coal. But then he was too old to hitch a ride on the mower and be King of the Castle. More of a dirty rascal.

"You're better off without the pills," Shani told him, just last week, after Double English. Lobo wanted to say, *"I'd be better off with you."* But she was just kind. She didn't love him. Why would she, when there were guys who were so whole and solid in the world, they didn't even know what might be broken? And Lobo couldn't find anything to hold on to that didn't shake and fracture, except her.

Outside the shop, Old Dope Head stood, looked at his phone and jerked to the right as if someone had pulled his lead. There were shakers who liked to rattle people and laugh at them, and Lobo had an idea this was one of them. Not a gardener at all. More of a night-time poacher like in stories, the kind who'd twist the rabbit's neck and keep sucking his mint without a pause of the tongue.

"What do you mean, vegan?" the nurse asked, but Lobo wasn't going to explain. Someone had to save the world.

Mrs Jennings appeared from the back of the shop. "Still quiet, then, Louis?"

For a moment Lobo thought she was accusing him, like the teachers in every report he'd ever had, so he nearly said yes, he intended to stay quiet for the rest of his life because shouting did his head in. Then he said yes, it was.

"Interesting-looking man," she added. "I don't know where he gets that energy from. A Marathon runner, I shouldn't be surprised."

Thinking about the customer who got away (fast) made Lobo really tired so he went to put the kettle on. Mrs Jennings reckoned he made a lovely cup of tea.

*

Roger hoped the 10:24 wouldn't leave a minute early again. He'd meant to take that minute off his walking time from gate to station but the in-growing toenail was giving him gyp. On her way out to her pre-school after breakfast, Maureen had told him not to worry because they couldn't manage without him 'at that office of yours' and everyone knew it. As if she had the faintest idea what the job entailed, or what – sometimes who – made it hell. "Roger's in Finance," she told people, leaving them to fill in the gaps if they weren't too bored to bother like her. Because deep down, in spite of the encouragement, she despised any work that wasn't 'human'. Roger wasn't sure at this point which of them had stacked up the most resentment – Maureen on account of the earning chasm, or him, the one she called her 'other half'. It seemed to him she only had to clean from infant bottoms what he had to wade through daily, right up to his ironed collar.

Advancing up the hill towards Roger was the type their daughter would call a hipster. A hippie-mod-geezer type who kidded himself he was nineteen in spite of the white beard, and tried to prove it by power walking. It had always galled Roger that some men sailed through life with no pressure, collecting benefits and then sitting outside the pub at night, beer on their top lips as they watched the commuters filing home. This one had never worked in an office, lucky bastard. Maybe he'd been a hod carrier on a building site, baring his chest, whistling at women and smoking his way to fitness. Secondary modern types like him had lain in wait for the posh boys after school, fags lit and knuckles ready.

Roger thought it must be his sixtieth birthday on the horizon dragging back the past to get in the way on a daily basis. And now he seemed to be in Hipster's way as the pavement narrowed. The pair of them jigged, but only one of them had snake hips: the same one who found the whole thing amusing: "Whoah there!"

Roger had been some kind of joke all his life to Hipster's sort. He was the kind they called cool and he'd know it. There was something devil-may-care in his red socks and boy jeans. No shortage of women for men like him, no headaches or tiring days at work to get in the way. "You need to lose some weight," Maureen said, at least once a month, year after year. "Haven't you had enough?" she'd ask, when he wanted seconds or needed toast before bedtime. He'd had too much of most things really, including her stories of funny things the little ones said, and the funny things she never tried to say herself any more. And *it*, with her. 'Sad or what?' he imagined Hipster saying, arm in arm with what Roger's dad used to call a 'buxom wench', a tart with dyed hair, caked eyelashes and a tight top squeezing up flesh.

Turning, he saw the man bend with the corner, rubbery and lithe.

Roger's watch told him the pavement tango had probably cost him that train and Hipster wouldn't care. Since he had zero chance of catching that scrawny neck to wring it, he might as well invest in hot chocolate, with whipped cream on top.

*

Kev liked to walk the first couple of miles and bus the rest. It was a slippery slope and he was trying to keep off it while he could. "Sixty-six!" people cried, disbelieving, but only because of the pace he kept up, and the jeans he could still zip. A few months' slobbing and his body would look as ancient as his beard. Kev didn't wear a watch anymore but he was good at time. That might be because he valued it now, much more than he used to when there was a wages slip each week as compensation for all those hours lost. With Bowie gone … well, it was a reminder to live. Joie de vivre was in short supply but these days he felt a hit of it each morning, especially Wednesday. He'd make it to the bus stop by the cemetery in time to catch the 10:32 and be at the café a minute or two before eleven.

Some of the guys were regular and that had to mean it was working. Jeanie too, doing well off the booze; she was starting to risk eye contact now. It was no use having goals like companies – or kids in school; that seemed a crying shame. People learned what they wanted to, and did what they chose with it. And if in this case, the target of the enterprise was non-profit, bullseye! Mal was achieving that big time, soft git, with what Kev called the *caff* and Mal called the *project*, bless him.

Mal knew the score; someone said he'd been 'inside' as a youth. That would make the do-gooding his penance. Then again, the other story doing the rounds had Mal ordained, with a dog collar in a drawer at home. Kev was willing to buy both or neither but Mal was making magic now either way. "What's in it for him?" Kev had wondered, first of all, when he heard about the community café. And the answer had seemed hard to believe – until he signed up to be a part of it, gratis unless you counted as much coffee and toast as he could handle.

Basic skills were about all Kev could teach when it came to numbers and words. But if they fancied making something with their hands, some wood and a few tools, then that was a whistling thing, a chatting and listening thing. And a quiet thing too, if they wanted it that way, with the scent, the grain and the texture to keep things sweet as the sawdust gathered around them. The first thing they had to overcome was fear of failing and Kev could help with that because he'd failed at most things on his way through. Keeping a marriage together, protecting the kids from shit, getting a foot on the property ladder: enough failure for an England team and it didn't stop him.

"You found your feet, Kev," Sharon said, after his first time. She was smart, too smart to be with him but maybe if he asked, she'd take him on a permanent basis. Give him a chance to get it right. He would have liked to find her something sparkly. He must show her how much he thought of her, same as the volunteers had to show the clients on Wednesdays. It made a difference, helped people see their way ahead without looking down at their shoes. And they all liked his: "You got your blue ones today!" and "Denim Kev!" as much as his shirts: "What's he wearing now?" or "Going to a fancy dress party after?"

Kev saw the bus coming. Moments later he'd swung up and paid his fare, found a seat and started up a conversation. Old ladies took a fancy to him, probably thought he was eighty too but charged up with Prozac. He couldn't help smiling at a baby on his mother's shoulder, meant to be sleeping with the movement of the bus but wide awake, eyes big. Kev had tried to be a good dad in the early days, wheeling the pushchair around the town till eyes like those closed. But howling was easier to stop than other kinds of trouble and he never meant to let anyone down.

He was old enough to do better now. Second chances weren't so much to ask and he'd be a real storybook grandad if they let him: funny, encouraging and patient too. He was getting good at all that, thanks to Wednesdays. "You're a good man, Kev," Mal told him last time, and Wilf echoed it, "Good man, Kev, good man, Kev." *"Yeah, one day a week,"* he'd thought. But it was a start. If Sharon called him a good man he'd probably break. That'd be too much happiness for one old heart, even a five star one like his that didn't need pills to help it out.

Kev looked out of the window at the street sliding by. It looked to him like the sun would be coming out any minute.

More about *On Track*

This is the most experimental of the stories here because there isn't really a story. What it offers, through a few minutes of time, is a series of encounters or observations. Three different people imagine for one striking individual an identity, a character, a life. In each case they read Kev through the lens of their own past, needs and feelings. In each case, as we discover when we see Kev from the inside, they're wrong. The idea for the story came from my own observation of a man very like Kev, seen from my window. I don't know who he is, or whether he would recognise himself. But imagining is part of a kind of reflex response we make to others. When I first started teaching, my flatmate and I often played 'Spot the Teacher' on the streets, the bus, the restaurant – but that's just a kind of Snap with stereotypes. Maybe those of us who construct characters and worlds for those unknown souls amongst us are the writers, actors or film-makers, and those who freeze time alone in forests or on mountains are the poets? Or maybe the reflex is not so big a jump from gossip.

I haven't seen the figure I named Kev since I wrote the story. So now I find myself developing a narrative to explain his disappearance ...

WOKEN

In the title story Woken, *the protagonist calls the close observation of the people all around him: "a breathing-in of the maximum air from other lungs." That's a spot-on description of Sue Hampton's own greatest strength: her almost preternatural ability to step into the shoes – the lives – of every character she introduces, large or small, every one of them as rich and real and secretly raw, as surreptitiously vulnerable, as any human being you've ever (or never) met. She is a sharp observer of the entire human experience, treating her creations with a remarkable tenderness and reverence even while she peels them to the bone. That's the kind of love one typically reserves for family -- and her ensemble feels in every way LIKE family, every character like a brother, mother, lover or son, so achingly familiar you want to hug them and shake them at the same time. In her latest enthralling anthology, Sue Hampton succeeds in doing what only the very best writers can do: transforming strangers on the page into people we know. Into people we are. Her fiction is a mirror held up to the human heart, and here we may all recognize ourselves. Another modern masterwork.*

Rick Cross, Alabama, USA, NASA media writer and author of *Times Squared*

Sue's work is dynamic, engaging and impossible to put down. Woken *beautifully confronts gender roles and provides a unique view of the social issues we face.*

Beth Garner, English teacher and organiser of the Women's March
on London, 2017

An incisive look at how the regular (but world-weary) folk of the world can find solace, through love and charity for our fellow human, and hope, through our shared resistance to an increasing hostile world.

Cllr. Matt Bradley, Deputy Head at St Luke's Primary School, London

WOKEN

No one saw it coming, apparently. Even Taylor didn't, not in any 3D sense. Like a dream, the idea held no sequence or shape.

It was a Monday in January, which didn't stop the South African flowers striking an exotic pose in the Partners' Lounge. Strellitzia, they were: a favourite of his mother's. Walking in, it had struck Taylor that in all that space they looked a bit like wind turbines in a field. Except that the City law firm's ambiance was a little more manicured and a lot less real.

Reality had left the building when they carried Col out on a stretcher. Col, who knew more about that building – and everything in it from the water cooler to the central heating to the photocopier – than Taylor would ever know about life outside. Without him the conditioned air felt sterile.

"This is about Colin, isn't it?" said Graham. "We're all still shaken but you two were pals …"

"Triggers aren't the same as causes," Taylor told him. "Causes have roots." He had a sense that in his case those were thick, deep and tangled.

"God, it's tragic," Harley muttered, a little breathy, with a few shakes of his head that made the expensively styled hair flop and swing. He pushed it back impatiently.

"Of course," said Serena, removing her glasses to look tender.

"Yes," said Taylor. "I went to see him in hospital last night."

Col shouldn't be there, not at fifty-five with early retirement in sight. Taylor remembered his dad's story of taking a radio to pieces, confident that he could reassemble it. Fooling himself. It was like that with Colin. He was no longer falling to the office floor with his coffee slapping the desk, but that didn't mean he was reconnected. And the only good man in the City deserved to outlive it.

Taylor answered questions that felt obligatory, conscious all the same that he was being rerouted. Did they think he'd rise any minute and return to his own office, as if to unsay the announcement that he'd finished with it, all of it, this fat living that was so much less than a life?

"How's Nina?" Serena jumped in sympathetically the moment he paused. "Back at work yet?"

"Tomorrow, she thinks." In fact in Nina's opinion, employment law should specify how many sick days could be justified by the death of a foetus not yet the size of a goldfish.

"For the best, I'm sure. She's not forty yet, is she?" said Serena.

"Ah, and your big 4-0 is looming large!" cried Graham, Archimedes-style.

"Yes," said Taylor. "That's one of the triggers, like the miscarriage and Col's stroke. But this isn't as sudden as it seems. Call it a year's sabbatical, if you like. I'll be a sleeping partner; the world is full of them. And Harry can take my cases; he's got the teeth. But don't count on me coming back."

There was silence then, before Harley's mobile rang, and he took it to the window where his back looked smooth but stiff. Graham glanced at Serena. Perhaps each of them was waiting for a cue from the other. But they weren't really in synch, the two of them, in spite of the rumoured affair. Not like Taylor and Col.

"I'll put it in writing," said Taylor.

As he turned into the corridor he heard Graham mutter, just louder than the stroke of his shoe on the new carpet, "For fuck's sake."

Taylor walked away imagining Serena's reassurance that it would blow over; he'd never follow through. Even though following through was as ingrained as the *work before sleep* expectation and the *partners as family* sham.

Closing the door in his own office, Taylor began to clear his desk.

When he arrived home just after six, Nina wanted to know what was wrong.

"I could say nothing and that would be a first."

"Some massive corporation," she guessed, sounding more tired than angry, "wants to buy your blood as well as your principles?"

She hadn't dressed or put make-up on, and he didn't blame her for that

109

but he knew it could mean she was feeling both vulnerable and angry about it.

"Not today. Or tomorrow either." He asked how she was. She didn't answer but said she hadn't got round to cooking anything yet.

"No need," he said. "Let's go out."

"We're not celebrating, Taylor," she pointed out. "At least, I'm not."

Taylor tried to hug her but she extracted herself, the furry belt of her wrap-around dressing gown falling to the floor. When he picked it up she didn't thank him, just slotted it through the loops. He saw the way she left one hand for a few moments on the stomach that had barely rounded.

Her flyaway hair looked tangled and lacklustre but he thought better of suggesting she washed it. Now he wasn't sure how to tell her. Was it terrible timing or the best? Hadn't she always hated having to settle for the sliver of Taylor Fordington that the law firm left for her?

"I have something to tell you," he said, as gently as he could.

"You're having an affair?" she suggested, and her pale face wore a brief smile while his protested. "I kind of hoped you might be," she added, the disappointment audible. "Because I think we should break up. I'm going to stay with Gemma and the kids for a few weeks and then I'll start looking for a flat." She turned away to reach for a bottle of red from the wine rack, and then the opener from the drawer. "Don't sweat over the financial side – I never wanted your money."

A get-out clause, he thought, remembering that she'd been adamant that joint accounts never worked. But how did he feel? Shouldn't he know, after four years and a semi-planned if very short pregnancy?

She poured two glasses while he watched silently.

"Is this what you need?" he asked as she left his on the worktop and began to drink her first alcohol since the blue line on the kit. "Space, I mean, not the booze."

"I don't know," she said, her voice thin enough to shatter. "But I know I don't need you. I'm sorry. I want you to be happy."

So he told her he intended to be, and explained about work. Nina was almost disbelieving. Then he read the hostility in her neck and shoulders even before she made a fist beside her glass on the kitchen table.

"But until today you couldn't even get home in time to eat together, never mind a movie or the theatre. You couldn't promise a garden on a

Saturday and if you did you broke it. You couldn't even stay with me when the spotting started – because the client mattered more than any baby we might make."

"I know. I'm sorry. I woke up." He reached for her arm where it looked so thin at the wrist, but she lifted it as she stood.

"Too late, Taylor," she said. "You won't change just because you have a guilty idea you should."

He didn't say he loved her. How long since he'd used the word? Blue line day, eleven weeks ago? If he did, it would only be because he had a guilty idea he should.

"And I don't love you," she said, eyes on the gleaming red in her glass. "I'm not sure I ever did and I want to find out what that feels like." She placed a hand on her belly again.

"So do I," Taylor told her, and this time she let him hold her.

That night she slept in the spare bed and next morning he stirred at the sound of her heels on the drive. Almost eight o'clock! Taylor heard the engine and rolled sleepily onto his front. It was closer to ten when he woke again and found she'd gone, not just to work but for good.

Good luck with the mid-life crisis. I'll drop by sometime for the rest of my clothes and a few bits so put a red hands-off symbol on anything you'd fight me for and you can save yourself the trouble. Happy to stay friends if you are. I'm not sure we were ever much else. XX

Taylor dropped it into the recycling, considering it evidence that Nina had always been – setting aside her earning power which was some thirty percent of his – way too good for him.

Delaying the inevitable with his parents as long as circumstances allowed, Taylor sent his sister Mila a text at what he thought might be playtime at her primary school. Still, he guessed she was probably spending it drilling the staff over how to please Ofsted.

But *Jacked in the law and the rat race to get a life and hunt my soul down* drew a welcome surprise:

YAY! About time. You did have one. I keep trying to drown mine when it rises up like a corpse from a lake and puts me off the data. Come to Sunday lunch. XX

He wasn't one to drag up childhood memories as if life used to be golden; Mila would be the first to agree kids could be shitty too. But over real coffee – two mugs of it – he turned the pages of his gran's old photo album, and smiled at himself, aged six or so, hand in hand with Mila on a white beach while she held her flowery sun bonnet in place; at the two of them even smaller and clowning in a tumble on a sofa; at a studio photo in which he played a responsibly custodial big brother, his jacket sleeve folded around her and his expression almost cleared of the usual amusement. Suddenly he remembered the trouble they'd given the photographer because such seriousness was hard to hold without spluttering. Was it part of the golden illusion or did he used to be fun?

There was a big photo of his parents dressed up for some expensive occasion, his mother's dress full-length and shiny silver and his father in a suit that could be Savile Row. Even though he only saw them around once a month, he'd hated them full-time, as a teenager pressurised to work for exams that seemed pointless. Hadn't his father's life ever made him want to wail or kick something, or leave his perfect shoes on a shore and keep swimming?

As for his mother, she was like a tasteful dressing table from another age, with several elegantly curved drawers that were hard to prise open.

Taylor closed the album. The chill winter sky made him think of platinum. He wondered whether Nina had left her ring.

What now?

For a few days he slept, read or at least sampled unopened books chosen for him over the years, made himself porridge and toast and ordered Indian takeaways, kept his phone off and avoided news in all its forms. He sat at the piano and emptied himself in the hope of making space for the schoolboy who reached Grade Five to return by time machine, to occupy his fingertips and stir the dead. But there was no resurrection, just a chain of chords with broken links: the soundtrack of waste, of conviction lost.

Taylor dressed only for daily ventures outside. The air was sharp, the surfaces slippery and the traffic constant but he couldn't be juddered any more than poisoned or upended, not now. He needed to focus on the green, however straggly, oppressed or thin it might be, on trees breathing life. Not litter or poverty, not fear or hostility in human eyes. Not the gulf between him and his gated home and the unwashed, uncombed guy who might have slept in a doorway and searched the bins for breakfast.

At the National Gallery he strolled, looking left and right like a pedestrian about to cross the road, stopping only when arrested by something he could name – or maybe only feel. Then he'd make notes and frame the image in his head with more insight than a raised phone ever managed, trying to absorb whatever it was that made him care. Knowledge and understanding were such different things and maybe connection was another, a step beyond either but a pre-requisite too, breathing life like the trees.

At the British Museum he looked for rooms, cultures, artefacts he didn't recognise. Like a tourist he sought out cathedrals, mosques, temples. Walking, he hoped for shoots, buds or birdsong breaking through. When he found the text about Col's complications and the hospice, he hardened so the tears wouldn't take him somewhere he couldn't leave. Back home he looked up the address but it was a time for family, surely. He'd send a card.

By the end of the first week he'd signed up for a course in World Religions and another on Art History. In the old-style paper diary he'd bought from Oxfam he'd written a few events with question marks: a community choir, a refugee support group, even a Knitathon for the Homeless where beginners were welcome. He'd left the cleaner a note about a fifty percent rise, donated some cans to the foodbank and wondered whether it was possible these days for a man to volunteer in a primary school to hear kids read without being liable to an MI5 stake-out.

"How are you feeling?" Mila checked most evenings. Taylor had a number of answers: "Good, great," "Just adjusting, reframing," or, "Alive. I'm awake." He told her Colin was apparently hanging on.

With his parents he decided a letter was best. Like any ex-boarder from the pre-text age, he'd mastered the art of evasion, euphemism, padding and non-news packaged with affable formality. They'd infer that he wasn't working just now but be none the wiser about why, or any intentions he avoided expressing. The break-up with Nina and the assumptions they'd be bound to make would serve as a distraction. Then one day, before too long, he'd talk to them – when he had words they would know how to receive. In the meantime, he assured them that he was under Mila's care. That would spare them panic. Mila, the sensible little sister who'd cry, as she giggled, "No, Taylor, stop!" because somehow she knew where 'too far' began.

"Come and stay," she told him now.

But it turned out she was too busy, what with school policies to update and her own two girls to steer past the glitter miniskirts towards dunga-rees, Lego and Doc Martens.

"Soon," she said. "Hold on, Taylor."

"Hold on?" he cried. "I'm floating. I'm high, baby! I'm on the breeze."

And the breeze was inside him. He didn't mind its bite, as long as he felt it – not just in his hair, lifting it like wings, but deep inside.

It was January 15th when he arrived at the church hall to deliver a sleeping bag Nina hadn't taken with her, one good pair of gloves from a nest of them, and a plaid Christmas scarf he didn't like. The women in charge of receiving and sorting were young and energetic. Everything they did was fast, including their words of welcome and thanks.

"Where will it all go?" he asked.

"To a warehouse, then by container wherever it's needed. We have an appeal for medical equipment for Syria too." The speaker had a huge weight of curly red hair, freckles and an accent that might be Italian. She indicated a money tub as she pushed clothes down into a bin liner. "Can you stay and help for a few minutes?"

"Sure. But are there any hospitals left – in Aleppo?"

"Look," she said, beginning to label the bag but stopping to look up, her green eyes fixed on him now, "we can't give up. God knows. One force or another might bomb anything we buy on Day One. That's beyond our control. We can only do everything we can."

Was she exasperated? He couldn't tell. "Yes," he said. "Power to you."

"Power?" she said, reaching for tape. "Isn't that the cause of all this? Screw power, yeah? The only power I recognise is love."

Taylor had no answer to that so he just nodded, and said, "I'm Taylor and I've got plenty of time."

She introduced herself as Francesca and explained the principle behind the sorting. Targeting the heaviest bags, he did his best, rejecting the damp or pungent stuff, throwing anything stained onto a mountain labelled unfit and joking about belonging there himself. The work was physical; his forehead soon began to sweat. He caught himself puffing and grunting. Then, when he found a plastic machine gun amongst some very third-hand toys, he let loose an expletive.

"Sorry," he said in the silence, and grabbing a naked Barbie by the leg, pulled a sideways face before repeating the word.

Francesca laughed. "A legitimate response, Taylor. On the shit pile please!"

"Ah," he said, looking at its label. "Cockney rhyming slang."

He wasn't sure she understood that, but one of the others grinned.

"But it's mostly good, like people," said Francesca.

"Wish that was my experience."

"Ah, with fat cats, maybe?"

Taylor didn't like the idea that it showed. He realised Francesca could almost be his daughter. So where had it come from, this certainty that had eluded him all his life?

He stayed long enough to help load a couple of vans.

"Is there a committee?" he asked a tiny young woman with cropped, pale blue hair.

"The next meeting's on Thursday morning," she told him, and pointed to the coffee shop opposite. "If you're free. Nine o'clock."

He nodded, resisted an urge to miaow his goodbye, and strolled away.

On the phone later, Mila told him not to fall in love. Taylor protested.

"It's goodness you're chasing," she said.

Taylor didn't answer. In the silence he heard her triumph. "All right," he said. "Smartass."

"But they don't need a Chairman," she pointed out. "Sounds like they're doing all right." He agreed. "What about you?"

"Oh, you know," said Taylor. "Finding I can live without saucers of cream."

So she told him to find a counsellor, which left him suddenly vague. Afterwards, stirring some scrambled eggs, Taylor smiled. Chasing goodness? Falling in love? He guessed he'd lost sight of the former when he outgrew Thomas the Tank Engine. And he wasn't sure he'd even trialled the latter. Otherwise he'd be weeping now, instead of rising each morning with a sense of mystery, discovery; a new tenderness. Maybe he was transferring to the world the care the baby would have needed, and maybe the world needed it even more.

But what about Col? Looking at the kitchen clock, Taylor calculated that he could get to the hospice by seven. He'd like to know how Col kept his soul intact all those years, surrounded by alligators in a swamp and without keeling over at the stench.

The hospice was old but colours and textures hid the cracks. Summer would have made a difference, offering flowers through windows. Now it was dark and chill, the driveway shiny white with frost. Taylor realised he should have brought something; Nina would have made suggestions. But could Col even turn the pages of a magazine?

Signing in, he was directed.

"There's another visitor there just now," said the guy at the desk. The whole package was so upbeat that Taylor didn't know whether he admired or hated it: the smile, the lift of the notes in his voice, the unbeaten frame of him as he leant back in the swivel chair. But what was the option? Wasn't he chasing goodness too? "No worries, it's Kat," he added. "The daughter?"

"Ah yes," said Taylor. According to Col, she worked at saving the planet with lentils and quinoa, a canal boat and a bike. So she wasn't blocking a fracking lorry just now.

Along the corridor and around the corner he found the room. Through the open door, he saw some kind of hardy evergreen outside, looking in and shivering its leaves through the glass. Taylor was glad to notice. It felt like learning to read.

Everyone in the building must notice Kat. Her dark hair made a bumpy little cap with lime-green fringing, and her coat, folded over the armchair, was patchwork velvet. Like the white mum she'd already lost to cancer, she was paler than Col. As she leaned towards her father, who lay still in the bed with the faintest trace of a rhythm lifting his chest, a long rainbow scarf trailed down over her knees to the floor. She smelt of something: sandalwood, maybe?

"I'm Taylor …"

"I know. Hi. Sit."

He insisted she stayed where she was and pulled over a plastic chair from the corner by the window. The street lights blinked through the branches.

"Hey, Col," he said, once seated.

"I've been talking to him too," said Kat. "Reminding him of things – you know, happy things. Loving him, really. Go ahead."

"We all trusted him," he told her, "way more than we trusted each other."

"That's sad," she said, "and a bit shameful."

He looked down at her red lace-up boots as she swung a denim leg.

"He helped me find my way around when I was new and green," he began. "That's not in the political sense."

"Really!" She was teasing.

"He had – has – the best smile." He'd never thought until he said it. The words felt heavy, ached. He looked to the bed. "I wasn't always free enough with mine. Too time-needy for smiling. I'm sorry, Col."

"You can hold his hand," she said, letting go. "Sit here and touch him. That may be the only thing that counts."

Taylor didn't argue. It felt awkward at first, reaching over and judging the thinness of the arm under the bedding. The hand felt cool.

"You made him laugh," Kat said, from the corner. "Taylor Boy, he called you."

"Yeah, the big kid."

"So what changed, with the time pressure?" she asked. "Because you're here now. I mean, is it only this – Dad, the hospice – or you too?"

Taylor hesitated. More information than she really needed? "Oh … Col, me, the world on fire …"

She nodded. "Look," she said, "why don't I get us both a coffee? Then you can be yourself for Dad without me earwigging, confess your sins." She stood. "But a few jokes wouldn't go amiss when I come back. We're a bit laugh-needy so far."

Taylor smiled. "No promises." But maybe he should have made more, and kept them too. Love was meant to be a promise, wasn't it? Not a speculative, see-how-it-goes suspicion, squaring up expenses with a suitcase close enough to grab from under the bed. Not littered with clauses making threats respectable.

He watched Kat walk away, the jeans sagging a little on a girl's bottom.

Ass would be her word for it. FRACK OFF was knitted into the back of her jumper. Nearly forty years on this earth and Taylor had never slept on a canal boat.

"You're proud of her, Col," he murmured.

Colin's forehead looked smoother than it used to. Taylor would hardly have known him without a smile. It left him older. His skin was less vivid, the brown more matte. Maybe only the body lived on, and the rest ...? The World Religions course would have some ideas and they might be fairy tales but sometimes disbelief was worth suspending.

"Women know what really matters." He remembered Serena, and the contempt that could cut like a laser. If Serena had ever known, she'd forgotten, the way he'd erased his French.

Taylor looked around the room at the cards, paper towels, tissues and wash basin, at COLIN and an illegible surname in red marker pen on the board above his head. If he'd really cared for this man lying here, he would have told him the shit behind office doors went deeper than he'd dream, and he'd be better off oiling a cleaner, greener machine – a school or a Civic Centre. A hospice.

Colin breathed a sudden, thicker breath, spiky as a doormat. It broke the barely perceptible rhythm and left a single twitch of his top lip. Taylor remembered how his laugh sounded, big in all that elegant space. At Taylor Boy, the funny one? Was that all he was?

"I've cut loose," he said. "Mila says I'm looking for love but I don't mean computer dating. The L-word – it's bigger than that."

Was that a smile, a trace of one? Couldn't be. A nurse knocked once and walked in, checked Col's pulse and read his temperature in his ear.

"Doing fine, Colin. You breathe easy. You've got people who love you and that's all anyone can hope for." She glanced up at Taylor. "Relative?"

"Friend." He amended it for accuracy. "Colleague." No need to amend that just because Colin had no Law degree.

After the nurse left, Taylor remembered something. He was in the middle of telling a Buddhist story he'd come across on Facebook when Kat walked in and smiled. She put down two coffee cups. He felt self-conscious now, and stopped.

"So everyone said it was bad luck when the farmer's horse ran off," she continued, "good luck when it came back with a wild horse tagging along, and bad luck when the wild horse kicked the son and left him limping. But when war broke out, the son wasn't fit to fight. Bloody good luck for him and everyone who loved him."

She looked at her father and stroked his forehead. Then she walked around the bed with Taylor's coffee.

"Your bad luck is good, right, Taylor?"

"I think so."

"Cool." She glanced back at the bed. "I'm happy for you. Did the rat quit the race? Tired of losing?"

"Tired of winning too." He grinned. "I'm sorry I haven't made you laugh."

"You're a different kind of funny."

She was a different kind of beautiful, he thought, and wondered how she'd react if she could read his thoughts. "Have you got plans after this?"

"I'm going on the Women's March on London," she told him, "next Saturday, after the Inauguration of the Beast. Come along. Unless you have the smallest moment of time for any one of his racist, sexist, homophobic, climate-wrecking oil buddy lies."

Taylor didn't suppose he did, not now – even if the Beast needed legal representation to sue someone over something on his Scottish golf course. "All right," he said. "Is it bad news that turns out good?"

"Yeah, if all over the world people of goodwill unite, in peace and in their millions, to disempower him. Dad would be proud of you, Taylor."

Taylor nodded.

"Dad," said Kat, looking at her father and touching his arm. "I like him too."

It was unsettling. At his evening class Taylor found it hard to pay attention even though Islam was quite a revelation when he did. Kat liked him. And he hadn't been so pleased about that since the school disco at the Prep, when all the girls wanted to dance with him and a few of them planted kisses on his cheek. But if Kat had been there, she'd have been the exception. She'd have danced on her own as if no one was watching, and even though some kids might have laughed at the wildness of it, he would have watched all right.

His number was on her phone but she hadn't given hers – keeping the locus of control. And she wasn't on Facebook to be friended. He looked up the march, which was meant to be a global protest about the rights of all people and the planet. She knew how fat the cat was, and how obese the clients, but she didn't question his credentials and he called that generosity.

A few days later he'd heard nothing. His piano wasn't progressing as fast as he'd hoped and although it was Thursday he wasn't sure about the refugee charity committee. Wouldn't Kat say he should spare them the patriarchy? He donated two thousand pounds anonymously through their website and waited for the sun before walking to the park to people-watch. To belong, really. He was pretty sure Kat wouldn't want to belong to anyone.

Saturday morning was frosty again. The march was due to start at the U.S. Embassy at twelve. What if he didn't hear from her? Would he really drag himself up there on his own, a first-timer out of his depth, if she didn't like him enough to hold his hand?

The text arrived when he was shaving. *Taylor Dad's gone. No marching for me. Tell me all about it.*

Oh God, thought Taylor. A corpse in a bed. The hand he pictured now was hers, holding the one with no movement, its heat ebbing away. Would her crying be silent?

She needed him to tell her all about the march and their talk would be real. When she was ready, he'd listen.

Another text, but this time from Mila: *Was aiming to bring the girls up to London with banners and pussy ears but logistics defeated me. What are you up to?*

Going up to London with no ears but I'll be the fattest cat, cream oozing out of my ears. X

On the station platform he spotted Francesca with a rolled-up banner next to a couple of other young women, a baby in a sling and some pre-school kids in trapper hats. Taylor raised a hand but she looked at him blankly for a moment before she gave him a thumbs-up. Suddenly he realised the refugees could have a coat, an expensive one, good as new. And shoes – how many pairs did two feet need?

There were pairs of mature women too, plus a couple of husbands. One had penned *LOVE* across her forehead under her white hairline and

120

rainbow striped hat – as if complicit in the ongoing conspiracy to lob that word at him from all directions. All right, he thought, enough. But then he supposed that with love that was the point; you couldn't have too much. And today was not the time to blame his mother, who'd missed that point, and never read the definition, probably because her own parents hadn't lived it.

No one asked, waiting on the platform or stepping into the same carriage, "Are you going my way?" or even gave him a smile of recognition. He supposed no one would suspect.

On the journey he decided to focus on the view from the window: the beauty along with the crassly disfigured, the grass and concrete, bushes, factories and trash. The materials and the way they absorbed or rejected sunlight; the smallest shift of frosted leaves framing a steep bank down to a steel fence; the roll of vehicles like ball bearings trying not to chink. Birds: flashes like brushstrokes on a vast canvas, then lost and untraceable, free.

He used to like the countryside as a boy, before it shrank to eighteen holes. Wondering whether Kat meditated, he imagined her by the hospice bed. How long did mourners get and could it be too much as well as too short? Taylor had been at boarding school when his grandparents died and he didn't remember even being told about the funerals. But emotional neutering must be a prerequisite for fat cats and he wouldn't be surprised to see the theory aired, one way or another, on a placard in Trafalgar Square.

Finding himself, at different times on the underground route, next to hatted protesters wrapped in scarves, Taylor kept himself separate and unidentified. They'd be surprised. And he didn't know why he reserved that distance, except reluctance to narrow options. Another get-out clause – when he could have said at any point, "Shall we dance?" because really he could still be the boy at the Prep School disco if he shed the skin that had thickened around him with the Burberry overcoat.

On Oxford Street the shoppers and marchers wove together in strands. *Misters for the Sisters* was held by a couple of cool-looking smart guys with American grins, but around him most messages hung low, and he was just thinking of swords in their scabbards before the fray when one was lifted high and spun, declaring *PEACE* as a sign on a blue and green earth. Out of step, Taylor, he told himself. Too male, man.

He'd seen enough demonstrations online to notice the difference around him. Policing was minimal and he heard no shouting. Arriving at Grosvenor Square, he smiled at all the bobbing pink, pretty much all of it worn by women who'd choose climbing walls over makeovers for their daughters' parties. The place was like the kind of quilt Kat would have on her bed, with every colour and pattern and all of it bright. Raised up now, the slogans were mostly home-made, some with care and flair that made him glad he hadn't bothered. Waved like flags, oversized painted vaginas made steely points, batting back the Presidential pussy boasts with a broad Shakespearian humour his mother wouldn't enjoy.

And there, just turning, was the Bard himself, dead right about such antics not making a man. In the same shot Taylor glimpsed a placard made from rough-cut corrugated card with the message *I am very upset* felt-penned with no frills, held by a girl who might be a student. So he should be. He was learning to be. He'd done World War Two for History A' Level, for God's sake – and enjoyed it more than the Maths, Economics or Business Studies.

From a stall under a green awning he heard, "Stand up to Trump badges, a pound," and found a coin that meant he did, would. No choice now. A few steps further on he signed a petition on a clipboard. Not that he'd seen many octogenarians minus Internet; the crowd was young.

Two women embraced with cries: "I can't believe it!" "I should've known you'd be here!" Was he the only Billy No Mates who'd come alone? Easing through spaces, he took in as many faces, jokes, pleas for *LOVE NOT HATE* and feisty rebellions as he could. It wasn't so much a kind of infiltrator's research as a breathing-in of the maximum air from other lungs. The guys here were decent, caring, keeping their fists in their pockets; the children weren't sour-faced or grizzling. It was cool, fun, a kind of carnival with the iron of conviction running through like scaffolding. No sign of heading off yet, but these people practised patience. There were whistles, thickening into a chorus and ending in a cheer. And he was smiling now, to be here.

"Hey, I'm from Gay ..." Taylor didn't hear the rest, but the young guy with a cameraman at his side was smiling too. "I'm mainly asking women, but can I interview you about why you're here?"

"Uh, sure ..." Taylor knew he should be used to thinking on his feet and flannelling convincingly. "But just for clarity, I'm not actually gay." And there was no chance to send another message: Taylor would like to withdraw his previous email. No highlight and delete.

"Sure, no problem." The guy's smile held, more or less.

At least, Taylor thought, he'd recalled *"You won't hold it against me?"* before it could air. Just the kind of routinely homophobic joke Harley and Graham would enjoy. "Sorry, dumbass straight guy embarrasses himself and looks for hole to fall through," he said. "You can do way better than me." He gestured around him. "Go on."

"No, you're all right, no sweat man. This is about unity, right – all of us, diversity and common humanity. That includes straights."

Taylor felt like he should be thanking him. "You're so right and I'm Taylor Fordington," he said. "Are we good to go?"

When his interviewer gave him a thumbs-up he looked to camera. Dignity, he told himself, however bad the case looks. Authority, sincerity … "I'm here because I was out of it, and I opened my eyes. I'm here because I met a woman who calls Trump the Beast and it's not a joke, it's a horror story. I'm here because I may have fallen in love with this woman, who can't be here because her dad died – like we'll all die, if we don't change the way we live together on this earth." He paused. "I've woken up."

The broader smile was reassuring. Nods too. A few people around him had listened in. He felt a slap on the back. "Congratulations!" he heard, and "Welcome to the resistance," and "Kat must be a great woman."

"Yeah," he said. He felt sixteen.

"Thanks, Taylor. That was cool. Invite us to the wedding, yeah? Look online tomorrow – hope Kat likes it."

Taylor thanked him. As the two guys moved on he found himself doubting, as he chatted with his neighbours, whether she'd hate it; whether she'd think him a juvenile fool, or the grandstanding manipulator the City had made him. Would she doubt too: whether his declaration was in fact fake, like the new News? And was he just swapping one role for another, to salve his conscience or get his leg over?

There was drumming now and he wouldn't mind feeling its rhythm close up, but first … Wouldn't she doubt he'd even be here? He drew out his phone for a selfie, with his badge and a crown of banners. There waiting for him sat a message, from her.

Are you really on the demo because I could meet you in Trafalgar Square around 4 after the speeches end. National Gallery, Van Gogh room?

He'd felt like this on a Sunday afternoon at boarding school, hoping his dorm-mate Charles would get a visit from his well-developed and big-haired sister. Until that first sighting Taylor had been exasperated with Charles for crying at night, until he reasoned that was fair enough because Taylor would have cried too, for missing her ...

I'm here. And it's good, literally. See you at 4.

A bit late for humour Taylor. There for real?

Seriously.

Taylor waited but maybe that was it, until four. He might have told her that that if he could be woken, then anything was possible, even a better world, and he might begin to believe it. But this wasn't about him. Squeezing into space, he smiled at a young child holding a placard up to his waist and chanting its painted message, "*Dump Trump, Trump is rude. Dump Trump, love is good,*" and nodding her head with such force that her plaits swayed. Her mum, who had a baby in a sling, smiled at her and then at him: my girl.

His phone, still in one hand, vibrated.

It's starting, Taylor.

Was it like a poem where every meaning counted? Standing still and thinking through all the ways he could reply he began a few, deleted.

I know, he told her, as around him the crowd began to move.

More about *Woken*

Years ago I went with Leslie to a City law firm to meet a man who had been at university with him, and contacted him having read his novel set in York in 69 (now called *Purple*). We were surprised by Henry's account of a kind of epiphany which took him in many of the directions I give Taylor as part of a search for meaning and a rejection of materialism and success. Leslie wrote a poem about it, which he sent Henry, but we heard no more from him.

Although I've drawn on my experience with People not Borders, Francesca and her friends are imagined. The scene at the charity collection for refugees is adapted – rather than taken – from life. But my fellow-Trustees inspire me in bigger, broader ways and know how much I love them.

Taylor is a fiction but the world around him is very real. I didn't know, as I began a story about awakening as a first step to redemption, that it would end at the Women's March on London after the Trump Inauguration – not until I'd marched. Rarely had anything felt so right. And I knew, whatever happened in America or beyond, that the story made an end to this collection, because the most stirring endings are always beginnings too.

ABOUT THE AUTHOR

Sue Hampton, happy these days to be known as the Bald Green Author, was born in Essex and now lives in Herts with her husband, Leslie Tate. Inspired by her father Paul, who was a poet, she wrote as a child and has never stopped – even through 19 years of teaching as a working mum to Philip and Sarah. Her first book for children, the historical adventure *Spirit and Fire*, was published in 07 and described by Michael Morpurgo as "enthralling ... powerfully written". It was the first of many as she now approaches 30 titles in print. Most are for children or teens, across genres, but Sue also writes adult fiction. *Ravelled*, her first short story collection, was published in 2016 and praised by authors, librarians and teachers. She is in demand as a visiting author delivering workshops in primary and secondary schools (600+), and as an Ambassador for Alopecia UK. You may have seen her lead a team of bareheaded ladies to a £29,000 victory for the charity on BBC *Eggheads*!

Sue writes because she's fascinated by people and loves to make an emotional connection with readers through her vivid characters. Sue also talks about being the living proof of the power of stories, because exploring her alopecia in writing changed her life. In her blogs she shares reasons to write, and bigger ideas about activism, diversity and individuality. *Traces* made the top three in The People's Book Prize 2012 and *Frank* won bronze in The Wishing Shelf Award 2013. Michael Morpurgo's verdict on *The Waterhouse Girl* was "beautifully written" and he called *Just for One Day* "terrific."

Sue is a Trustee of a small charity called People not Borders – supporting refugees any way they can – in her home town of Berkhamsted. Sue's interests include music from Bach to Stravinsky and Nina Simone to Radiohead via Bowie, along with ballet and modern dance, art and film. She's a Quaker and a member of the Green Party, Campaign Against the Arms Trade, Greenpeace, Friends of the Earth and CND, and loves forests, gardens, mountains and the sea.

http://www.suehamptonauthor.co.uk/

Acknowledgements

Thank you to my beloved husband Leslie Tate, who is a novelist and poet and without whose inspiration and support I would have given up writing long ago.

https://leslietate.com/

I'd also like to thank mixed-media artist Paula Watkins for the cover image which I knew was right as soon as I found it on her website: http://www.paulawatkins.co.uk/ and to photographer Paul Watkins who captured it so vividly: http://www.paulwatkinsphotography.co.uk/

I have to thank Mikaela Morgan: http://mikaelamorgan.co.uk/ for her portrait of me on the back cover.

Of course I'm very grateful to all my reviewers and to Anne Samson at TSL for her excellence and thoroughgoing niceness too, both of which make working with her a pleasure.

http://tslbooks.uk/

www.ingramcontent.com/pod-product-compliance
Lightning Source LLC
Chambersburg PA
CBHW070826250626
47170CB00006B/2222